MURDER
AT METROLINA

KATE MERRILL

BELLA
BOOKS
2017

Bella Books, Inc.
P.O. Box 10543
Tallahassee, FL 32302

Printed in the United States of America on acid-free paper.

First Bella Books Edition 2017

Editor: Katherine V. Forrest
Cover Designer: Linda Callaghan

ISBN: 978-1-59493-532-9

About the Author

Kate Merrill is an art gallery owner and real estate broker with a lifelong passion for writing. She lives with her family on a lake in North Carolina. When she is not writing, working with the art community, or selling real estate, she enjoys swimming, boating, and allowing her two strong-headed golden retrievers to take her for a walk.

www.katemerrillbooks.com
merrilljennings@aol.com

Dedication

For
Susan

Acknowledgments

Special thanks to
Linda Hill
and the staff at Bella Books,
Katherine V. Forrest
for her invaluable editing help,
and those friends
who encouraged me to give birth
to Amanda Rittenhouse.

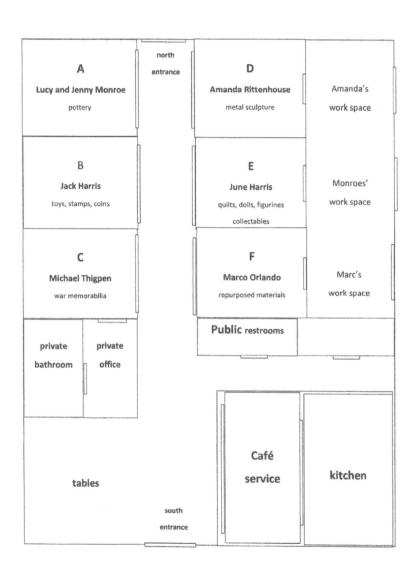

CHAPTER ONE

Who are these people?

AMANDA RITTENHOUSE was hyperaware of her mother's cool fingers looped around her wrist as they strolled arm in arm down a pathway lit by Tiki torches. Heading for a rustic clapboard shack called Buffalo Guys, they were sandwiched fore and aft on the narrow trail by the rest of the group, everyone laughing and talking at once, a gang of strangers. As she breathed the warm fishy-smelling air fogging up off the Catawba River, suddenly her mother's grip, even though it hadn't tightened, felt more like handcuffs than the tender gesture it was intended to be.

Their host and hostess for the evening, Trevor Dula and Ginny Troutman, led the parade. Trev, darkly handsome as a time-warped Elvis Presley, owned this music bar and restaurant, while Ginny, with her short black punk-cut hair, silver stud in her left nostril, had suddenly become Amanda's stepsister. Although Amanda sensed a kindred spirit in Ginny, who was exactly her age, she refused to even go there. To hell with relationships, family or otherwise.

Behind Trev and Ginny, Amanda's estranged brother Robby loped with his long-legged giraffe walk and glanced hopefully frontward and backward, seeking approval. It had always been that way. As children growing up in Philadelphia, even though Robby was two years her senior, he was the one who always sought to please. Now, at age thirty, his shy, introverted personality still made him seem like an overeager little boy. Unlike him, when their dysfunctional parents divorced, Amanda got the hell outta there, running away at age eighteen. In many ways, it felt like she'd been running ever since.

Her mother gave her wrist a little squeeze of encouragement, while right behind them Amanda felt the close, towering presence of Matthew Troutman, her new stepfather. She couldn't help but like Trout, as everyone called him. The man radiated warmth and stability. His gentle, reassuring ways were the polar opposite of Amanda's father, Robert Rittenhouse, the formal, uptight lawyer who had ruled their household with an iron fist. She wondered, not for the first time that week, how her cool and distant mother had hooked up with such a free spirit.

"How are you doing, honey?" her mother whispered into her ear.

Amanda glanced briefly into intense blue eyes, which were disturbingly like Amanda's own, and noticed the laugh lines and crinkles at the corners of her mother's mouth. They hadn't been there before.

"I'm fine, Diana." She hoped with all her heart that her mother noticed how she refused to call her Mother. The name Mother had to be earned, and as far as Amanda was concerned Diana had a lot of work to do before she got there. Perhaps the slight was cruel and childish, but Amanda couldn't help herself.

"Isn't it amazing, all of us together like this?"

"Yeah, it is amazing." She hadn't seen her mother or brother for ten years, so what else would it be but amazing? Bizarre maybe?

Bringing up the rear were the last two guests in their party: the crazy redhead, Liz McCorkle, who was her mother's real estate partner, and Danny Capelli, Liz's jolly fiancé, who was some sort of building contractor. The two were a little older than her brother, and she supposed they would be a fun pair to know, but they were so *southern*. Far as Amanda was concerned, this past week she had stepped into not only a surreal new family dynamic, but also a foreign country.

"Too bad your grandma and Linc couldn't have joined us," her mother said.

"Yeah," Amanda mumbled. That was another thing. Her grandmother Vivian, at age seventy-five, had caught the same disease afflicting the others and decided to get married. At this very moment, Grandma Viv was back at Trout's lake cottage with her boyfriend Lincoln, a white-haired gent pushing eighty. They were purportedly babysitting Ginny's seven-year-old daughter Lissa, but Amanda thought they were probably getting drunk on sherry and playing footsie under Trout's cocktail table.

"Well, here we are!" Trev flung open the door to Buffalo Guys, pride of ownership on his face, and they all filed into a dimly lit reception foyer.

Amanda was assaulted by the thudding bass of the country-western band playing on the stage near the bar. She felt it in her gut. She also felt peanut shells and sawdust under her feet. Mostly she was dumbstruck by the side by side images of her mother and herself reflected in the large gilt mirror across the room. At a glance, they appeared to be twins. Both were unusually tall, athletic and slim, with extremely short hair—her mother's pure white, Amanda's duck-down blond. They wore sturdy sandals, jeans and loose shirts untidily tucked at the waist. They posed with both hips cocked up on the left, bearing weight on their right legs, and they looked for all the world like the prelude to a vaudeville routine.

Her mother saw it too, and gave a little gasp of surprise as she released her daughter's arm.

"We'll eat on the deck, where we can hear ourselves think," Trev announced. And without further discussion he ushered them outside to a large porch hung above the river, where a picnic table was set for eight. "Have a seat, folks. Dinner n' drinks are on Ginny and me."

Amanda had assumed all the newlyweds and all the about-to-be-weds would cozy up side by side at the table. But instead they mixed it up, so that Amanda was across from Ginny, Liz and her mother. She could deal with the girls, but why was it so hard to look at her mother?

The waiter brought several pitchers of beer, with Bell jars to drink it from, as well as a choice of wines. Everyone cheered and studied their menus.

Mist lifted off the river. A new moon and first stars filled the cobalt sky. Amanda tuned out the chatter as everyone ordered, and then she slipped into her zone. This allowed her to quietly hover above the chaos, like the mockingbird singing in one of the dark, distant treetops. And from high above, she observed and wondered: *Who are these people?*

One week ago, she and the others had witnessed her mother and Trout's wedding at a rustic chapel in the mountains. She'd been summoned there by these voices from the past, and with her life already in turmoil, she had decided to come. Afterward she and her long-lost brother had camped out at their new parents' lake home, where they were encouraged to get to know this family of strangers—not to mention a motley collection of friends and dogs.

"I have to go back to Philly tomorrow," her brother whined at her elbow.

"Oh, I wish you could stay a little longer," their mother said.

Sneaking a peek at her mother's face, Amanda believed her entreaty was sincere, but would she be sorry when Amanda left? Her mother had always described how she and Grandma had fought. They were like oil and water, just wouldn't mix. But weren't she and her mother the same? Maybe fighting with one's mother was a family trait.

"I'll have the catfish platter with coleslaw," she absently told the waiter. Below the deck, she heard something large splash in the water.

"I'll bet you have alligators down where you come from," a male voice said from the end of the table.

Startled, Amanda realized Danny was talking to her. "Uh, yes. Even within the Sarasota town limits, they've been known to slither out of pools and eat the neighborhood poodles."

"Oooh, that's disgusting!" Liz made a face.

Still zoning, Amanda recalled that Liz and Danny were getting married this summer, as were Ginny and Trev, as were Grandma Viv and Linc. What was wrong with these people? Didn't they realize that commitment of any kind was a dead-end street?

"I have to leave tomorrow too," Amanda abruptly announced.

Her words sucked the sound out of the night. The birds stopped singing, the fish stopped splashing, even the band took a break.

"Why leave so soon, honey?" Her mother's pale eyebrows arched in disappointment. "We need more time to get to know one another again."

Right. Like that would ever happen. Why was everyone staring at her?

"C'mon, Mandy, you can't go yet." Ginny winked, causing the silver stud in her nose to bob. "I have plans for tomorrow, just you and me. You're gonna love it, I promise."

Was this a conspiracy? They all seemed to be hanging on her response, like if she said the wrong thing, their world would deconstruct.

"Well, girl?" Trout prompted rather sternly. "Do you have anything better to do?"

She thought about it hard, but no matter how she sliced and diced it, no, she had nothing better to do.

CHAPTER TWO

Fairground, or prison…?

"So, where are we going?" Amanda yawned as Ginny steered her forest green Subaru off River Highway onto Interstate 77 South, heading for Charlotte.

"It's a surprise. Relax and enjoy the view."

View? Amanda's idea of a view consisted of royal palms marching along a grand avenue lined with highrise condos and exclusive boutiques, like back home in Sarasota. Here the rural, sparsely forested fields were carelessly punctuated by new suburban shopping centers that had sprung up at each exit.

Ginny shrugged, noticing Amanda's skepticism. "Yeah, I know I felt the same way when I got here from Vegas. But the lake's pretty cool, right?" She nodded at the wide expanse of water opening to the right of the highway.

Amanda was forced to agree. "Sure, the lake is nice." Lake Norman had over five hundred miles of shoreline and stretched about forty miles north to south west of the interstate. Her mother the real estate broker said the lake was responsible for the area's recent prosperity, as well as the out-of-control growth.

Thousands of newcomers from all over the country had arrived, like her mother, to cash in on the potential.

"Did you enjoy the boat ride yesterday?" Ginny asked.

"Yeah, it was fun." Her mother's new husband had bought a pontoon boat as a wedding present to them both. Its maiden voyage the day before had been a long tour from the top of the lake around Statesville, all the way down to Huntersville, where a nuclear plant employed the cascading water to power all the surrounding communities. "I got sunburned though," Amanda added. She didn't want Ginny to misinterpret her enthusiasm.

Ginny laughed. "Yeah, you and your mother both. Did you see her nose at breakfast? God, you two are just alike with that fair skin. You burn if you get near a lightbulb."

"We are nothing alike," Amanda objected.

Her stepsister frowned and glanced at her from the corner of an eye. "Okay. Do you wanna tell me why you're so hard on Diana?"

A big cloud passed over the sun and long, finger-like shadows stretched across the road. Amanda stared at the stick-like trees making the shadows. "Hey, you didn't grow up with Diana."

"Hey, I wish I had a mother."

Ashamed, Amanda clamped her jaw shut so she wouldn't say something hurtful. She knew Ginny's mom had died of cancer, and Trout had admitted that he'd been so devastated by her death that he'd ignored Ginny, shut her out. He blamed himself for her running away from home at age eighteen, just like Amanda had done.

"Well, *I* love Diana," Ginny continued. "She's fun and funny. She's been great to Lissa and me, and terrific for Dad."

"I'm happy for you all." Amanda hadn't meant to sound so snide, but the past week in close proximity to her mother brought out the worst in her. All anyone talked about was Diana's witty sense of humor and her uncanny ability to solve murder mysteries, of all things. The brave, adventurous woman they described was no one Amanda recognized.

"I don't get your attitude," Ginny said. "Robby adores Diana. Did you see him this morning?"

Yeah, she'd seen her brother blubbering like a baby when the taxi came to take him to the airport. He didn't want to return to Philly and the law practice he shared with their father. Indeed, all Robby talked about was how he wanted to quit law and become a teacher, and Diana had encouraged him in his silly dream. But Robby had always been Mama's Boy, and Amanda had been Daddy's Girl. Always a tomboy, she'd played golf and tennis with her father. She'd gone fishing, hunting, even fixed cars with the man. When Diana divorced him, claiming Daddy had been violent and abusive, she didn't believe it, not for one minute.

"Mandy, I think you'd change your mind about Diana if you stayed a little longer. You should give her a chance."

Ginny wasn't going to let this go. Suddenly Amanda regretted delaying her departure by even one day. Also, she strongly suspected this mission they were currently undertaking was part of a giant plot to keep her here.

"So please tell me, where *are* we going?" she demanded.

"Like I said, it's a surprise. But since we're almost there, I'll give you a hint…"

Amanda noticed they had exited the highway onto Harris Boulevard. "So what's the hint?"

Ginny's dark eyes sparkled with mischief. "Well, you make sculpture, right? And you said you needed workspace and a place to exhibit, so I had this brilliant idea…"

"Not here in North Carolina!" Amanda snapped. Why on earth had she opened her big mouth and confided in Ginny? In a weak moment, just because they'd both been runaways and seemed to share a wild gene, she had let her guard down and confessed her passion for metal welding. Big mistake.

"Hey, maybe it's a silly idea," Ginny assured her. "Let me show you the place and if you don't like it, just say no. Nothing ventured, nothing gained."

Ginny slowed the car and drove into a large expanse of acreage surrounded by a tall chain-link fence. In the distance, Amanda saw two huge steel buildings that could have been armories or airplane hangars. These buildings were connected by a roofed, open-air pavilion with picnic tables. Beyond them, four tiers of smaller steel buildings, like enormous garages, marched into the barren fields.

They continued through muddy blocks of land devoted to parking for hundreds of cars, then up to a guard station, where a sleepy attendant glanced at Ginny's pass then waved them through.

The whole complex seemed deserted under the mid-May sun. Amanda blinked in confusion. "Is this a fairground, or a prison?"

"Neither." Ginny grinned broadly. "Welcome to Carolina's Metrolina Tradeshow Expo, one of the largest arts and antique shows in the country!"

CHAPTER THREE

Building 16...

"But where the hell is everybody?" Amanda wondered.

"My dear Mandy..." Ginny smiled indulgently. "It's a weekday in the middle of the month. Metrolina only operates for four days around the first Saturday of each month, and wait until you see it then, it's a zoo!"

"I guess I'll have to take your word for it." Amanda scowled as Ginny navigated past the two huge buildings, then turned right between the first rows of steel garages. She came to a stop at Building 16.

"This is your future, Mandy," Ginny exclaimed.

In that case, Amanda's future looked mighty bleak, because aside from a few cars parked randomly here and there, the place was more like a state fairgrounds after the exhibitors, carnival rides and laughing guests had long departed. "You've got to be kidding," she grumbled.

"No, wait until you see inside. Diana's partner, Liz McCorkle, gave me the pass and a key. She knows a woman who exhibits here and that woman told her there's space available."

"So you're all in on this?"

"Well, Diana and Matthew know. They really hope you'll like the place."

With no choice but to grin and bear it, she was determined to make this tour fast. "Okay, let's do it."

They crawled from the air-conditioned Forester into the heat, then walked up a short dirt pathway to a large, corrugated steel door. Amanda hoped that somebody would plant the sorry-looking flower boxes flanking the walkway with something colorful—impatiens or marigolds—because this first impression would scare the buying customers away. She noticed a billboard near the door listing the exhibitors within and wondered if anyone really made a living here.

When they stepped into the dim interior, Amanda heard the whir of overhead fans, which did little to cool the stuffy space. The building included an open hallway running the full length, with what appeared to be six large exhibit areas labeled A-F, three on each side. Most spaces were closed off by bright blue tarps hung down from the individual stalls, but directly to their right, in Space A, lights glowed and a radio was tuned to a gospel channel.

"Anybody home?" Ginny called.

After a flutter of activity, a round pink face peeked out from behind the tarp. "Oh, I didn't hear you girls come in!"

The woman was short and plump, with big brown eyes and a pageboy haircut. Clearly they had startled the poor lady, so Ginny quickly introduced themselves and stated their business.

"Oh, I see," she said. "I am Lucy Monroe…" She paused to stare suspiciously at Ginny, with her nose stud, tight red halter top and raggedy jean shorts. She looked more favorably upon Amanda, in pressed khakis and a baggy blue T-shirt.

"I know your mother, Diana Rittenhouse. She sold my house for me, and we got a good price too. Then her cute redheaded partner Liz found this adorable little townhouse for Jenny and me to buy in Huntersville. I just love those two, so y'all come in and make yourselves at home."

They followed Lucy into a spacious but crowded room filled with shelf upon shelf of handmade pottery. Amanda saw everything from wheel-thrown utilitarian vessels to distinctive face pots and imaginative slab constructions.

"You made all these?" Amanda was truly impressed.

"Yes, ma'am, me and my daughter Jenny." Lucy waved at a corner where a chubby teenaged girl was half-hiding behind a display of brightly glazed fantasy animals. She came out reluctantly and attempted a smile through a mouthful of silver braces.

"And I bet *you* make these." Ginny pointed at the animals. "I love them. They're so whimsical!"

Jenny looked to her mother for a clue as to how she should respond to such praise.

Eventually, Mom responded for her. "Yes, ma'am, Jenny makes the crazy critters from low-fire earthenware clay and paint-on glazes, while my stuff is high-fire stoneware. We have two kilns."

"But where do you work?" Amanda asked.

"Well, that's the beauty of this building, the feature that makes it different from all the others," Lucy said. "The whole east side is devoted to rough studio space. Three of us share it, but the girl who used to be in Space D, right across the hall from us, just up and left. One third of the studio space was hers."

"Oh really?" Ginny cast a meaningful glance in Amanda's direction. "So Space D and its studio space are available to lease?"

"You bet." Lucy nodded. "Wanna have a look-see?"

Amanda was getting excited in spite of herself, but she wasn't about to say so.

"We'd love to see it, if it's not too much trouble," Ginny spoke up. "My stepsister Mandy might be interested."

"Really?" Lucy gave Amanda a hopeful smile.

"Not really."

Lucy shrugged amiably. "Well, I'll show you anyway."

Too shy to tag along, plump little Jenny stayed behind as her mother opened the space across the hall and took Amanda and Ginny through it. Along the way, Lucy told them the long painful story of her divorce from an abusive husband named Jimmy and her hardships as a single mom.

Amanda tuned it all out, because the possibilities for Space D were endless. The dingy pegboard walls would sparkle with a fresh coat of white paint, and there was plenty of room for the largest of her welded sculptures—even for the funky furniture she had made from old tailpipes and auto bumpers.

"What do you think?" Ginny prompted.

"It's not too bad," Amanda conceded.

"C'mon, I'll show you the workspace." Lucy opened an almost-concealed door at the side of the room, and they entered a dark cavern. Then she opened an electrical box and tripped the switches, which flooded the long space running the full length of the building with intensely bright light.

"Wow…" Amanda breathed. "This is sufficient."

Ginny gave her an odd look. "I think she means the artists can see what they're doing."

"Well, we're not all *artists* here," Lucy said. "Jenny and me consider ourselves craftsmen, while the handsome hunk who trades in recycled building materials is more of a carpenter—even though he paints wild canvases," she added grudgingly.

Amanda took it all in. The room was casually divided into three sections. As she walked the length, she could not imagine what the girl who left Space D had done, because all she noticed in the broom-swept area were some brightly colored shards of fabric and yarn.

"Oh, she was a weaver." Lucy had read Amanda's mind. "She had a big loom set up back here, sewing machines too."

The boundaries of the potters' space were loosely defined by drying racks, with the potter's wheel dead center and the two kilns against the back wall. Lucy and Jenny Monroe also had a utility sink, which, Lucy informed her, they allowed the others to use. Their space smelled earthy, like wet clay.

The last area was obviously the handsome hunk carpenter's and seemed to be a chaotic pile of junk. Amanda saw old mantelpieces, sheets of bead board, ancient heart-of-pine flooring and antique bricks stacked randomly. One corner included a workbench and tools. Everything smelled of old wood, dust and lemon oil.

"Wow!" was all Amanda could manage.

"Interested?" Lucy pressed.

"Maybe we are," Ginny interjected. "How much does it cost?"

That would have been Amanda's next question.

"You should visit the Lease Office in the Main Building," Lucy said. "The Super's always on duty, and he'll give you a price schedule."

"Great! Let's go, Mandy."

Amanda felt a weird mixture of dread blended with hope. The combination made her woozy. "No, you go without me, Ginny. I'll hang out here and explore some more."

"Okay, be that way." Ginny stomped back through the door leading to Space D, while Lucy waddled behind, turning off the lights. "I'll get the damned price schedule!" Ginny called.

Amanda and Lucy watched her truck down the road toward the largest of the steel buildings.

Lucy turned to Amanda. "Do you want a complete tour?"

"No, thanks. I want a bathroom."

CHAPTER FOUR

A moment of epiphany…

"The restroom is down at the other end, to the right of the cafeteria, inside the private office," Lucy said.

"You have a cafeteria?" This place was looking better all the time.

"It's only open during the show weekends. They sell chili dogs, fries, greasy hamburgers—you know, junk food."

"I love junk food!" Amanda spontaneously admitted.

"Me too, can't you tell?" Lucy patted her fat tummy. She dug into the pocket of her floral housecoat and brought out a key on a short wooden baton. "This is for our private bathroom. It's not open to the public, and it's unisex."

"No problem."

"Of course, we have public restrooms behind the cafeteria, but they're locked during the downtime."

"I understand." Amanda took the key. If Lucy didn't let her go soon, she'd be in trouble. Suddenly the gallons of coffee she'd consumed that morning needed an outlet.

"Be sure to lock up when you're done," Lucy called as Amanda rushed down the hallway.

As she hurried, she sensed dark shapes looming from the exhibition spaces to either side. It was eerie, like trespassing in a closed museum, but this museum was definitely downscale. When she reached the end of the hall, she saw upturned chairs on the café tables and chain link pulled across the kitchen's service window. Finally, she found the office marked *Private* and the restroom inside. After a few fumbles, she unlocked the bathroom and gratefully sank onto the john. She found a dangling string, pulled it, and turned on a single bulb above a dingy sink.

She sat staring at the colorful ads for vintage merchandise framed on the walls and listened to birds flapping around in the steel rafters. She figured they'd flown in through the many open air vents she'd seen near the ceiling.

Soon Amanda heard another sound: heavy truck wheels on gravel. The vehicle came to a halt just on the other side of her flimsy wall. A key rasped in the lock of the corrugated steel door at this end of the building, and then she heard two voices, a man's and a woman's.

"Why do we have to unload today?" the woman complained.

"Why can't you just suck it up and help me with this?" he answered angrily. "We need to empty the truck so I can pick up another load tomorrow."

Amanda felt like a trespasser, an interloper. Should she hide in the bathroom, or step out and explain herself? As she held her breath, the doorknob a few feet from her nose suddenly jiggled, then turned.

"Oh my God!" She was completely exposed.

"Oh shit, I'm so sorry!" The man quickly backed away and closed the door with the universal speed of extreme embarrassment.

Amanda was mortified. She jumped upright and pulled up her pants. But of course it was too late, the damage already done. The intruder, obviously the handsome hunk carpenter, had gotten an eyeful. So had Amanda. She'd seen him shirtless, his narrow waist and rippling muscles, his startled brown eyes above a square jaw below a short buzz-cut of shiny black hair.

"Oh shit is right," she muttered as she caught the reflection of her flushed face and shocked eyes in the mirror. As she nervously washed and dried her hands, she now definitely wanted to hide here forever. In the meantime, she heard the man and woman whispering just beyond the paper-thin wall. Likely they were just as clueless as she was about how to resolve this uncomfortable situation.

Well, the choices being limited, Amanda figured she might just as well make the first move. Squaring her shoulders, she stepped through the private office and into the hall. At first the light pouring through the opened back door blinded her, but then she saw the couple standing side by side.

The sight froze Amanda in wonder. It was a rare moment of epiphany, for lack of a better word. The handsome young man was one pace behind the woman, in partial shadow, with only the planes of his cheekbones, biceps and edge of one leg illuminated, like the highlights in a Cubist painting.

But the woman was spotlighted in a conical beam of sunshine issuing from a ceiling vent. The golden glow was softened by shimmering dust motes. The beam glistened on her shoulder-length black hair, then cascaded like water over the gentle curves of her breasts and hips. But most dramatic was the oval of light that hovered like a cameo around her beautiful face, featuring her emerald green eyes and full red lips parted in a smile.

Amanda understood in those timeless seconds that this astonishing tableau would be etched in her mind forever. It stopped her breath and halted her heartbeat, until mercifully, the enchantment ended as abruptly as it had begun, and the world started spinning again…leaving the three of them staring at one another.

The woman spoke first as she stepped out of the spotlight. "Who are you?"

"Sorry about before," the man added sheepishly.

Completely disoriented, Amanda had forgotten about the embarrassing incident in the bathroom. Moving back inside her skin, she walked forward and held out her hand. "Amanda Rittenhouse," she automatically introduced herself.

The woman, who was about three inches shorter than Amanda, took her hand. Her skin was soft and warm, her handshake firm. "I'm Sara, and this is Marco."

"Marco Orlando, but everyone calls me Marc." The man stepped from the shadows and also shook Amanda's hand, but he held it a heartbeat too long. "I have the booth across the way, Space F."

Amanda worked to compose herself. The man's obvious interest made her uncomfortable. "Then you must be the antiques dealer. Lucy Monroe told me about you."

"Did she, now?" Marc took her elbow and guided her into his booth. "Come in. I'll show you what we do."

Sara followed and perched on a stool on the periphery while Marc explained the nature of what proved to be a fascinating business. Basically, the man traveled throughout the southeast salvaging materials from old residences, warehouses and barns being torn down. He rescued architectural elements like special mantelpieces, doors and window frames, floor and ceiling moldings. He saved unique flooring, bricks and paneling—anything of quality or aesthetic value—and then repurposed these materials into new construction.

"Think of it as recycling," he said. "We hate to see this stuff go to waste."

"So you use this booth as a showroom, and people can see what you do?" She wished he would let go of her elbow, so she deliberately moved away. At the same time, she was aware of Sara leaving her stool and joining them.

"One time Marc actually rented scuba gear and pulled some ancient logs from a river in Georgia. He had them milled into floorboards, and they've been a best seller," Sara proudly added.

Amanda was impressed. At the same time, she noticed an easel with an unfinished canvas propped in an inconspicuous corner. Her heart dropped. The last thing she needed in her life was another artist. She turned to Sara. "Are you the painter?"

The woman laughed. "God no, Marc's the painter."

"It's a hobby," he said. "Something to do while the browsers are here, wasting my time."

Amanda couldn't curb her curiosity. "Sara, do you help your husband with the business?"

Again the laughter. This time it was as raucous and deep-throated as the Liberty Bell—a big sound for a little woman. "Jesus, Marc's not my *husband*, he's my *brother*!"

"Oh." Amanda was relieved, in light of how Marc had been flirting with her. "So what do you do, Sara?"

She rolled her eyes. "Believe it or not, I'm a shrink."

"A psychiatrist?" Amanda was totally nonplussed.

"Yes, when I'm not helping my brother choose and haul his junk, I'm picking through the junk in folk's heads."

For once Amanda was at a loss for words. Luckily, they were interrupted by Ginny, who burst into the space with a wad of papers in her hands.

"Hey, what's happenin'?" she said.

Amanda introduced her, noting how Ginny's eyes clung to Marc, an inappropriately hungry reaction from a gal about to be married. Once Marc had repeated the spiel about his repurposing business, Sara again turned to Amanda.

"So what are you doing here at Metrolina?"

Before Amanda could respond, Ginny spoke up. "My stepsister's thinking about renting Space D. She's a sculptor."

"Really?" Marc and Sara said in unison.

"No, not really." Amanda could have murdered Ginny on the spot.

"No, you're not really a sculptor, or no, you're not really renting here?" Sara asked.

"No, I'm not really renting here."

"C'mon, Mandy. It's cheap, you won't believe it!" Ginny waved the lease papers in her face.

"Too bad." Marc looked crestfallen. "Maybe you should sleep on it?"

"Yeah, Mandy, you don't have to decide this minute," Ginny urged.

Amanda felt three sets of eyes boring into her. Damn it, they'd put her on the spot. "Okay, I'll sleep on it," she told them, and then walked purposefully from the building.

CHAPTER FIVE

The call at midnight…

Amanda couldn't sleep on it, because she couldn't sleep at all. Whether her insomnia was caused by the Carolina barbeque and hush puppies uneasy in her stomach, the haunting image of Sara and Marc in the sunbeam, or the dread of Robby's phone call—she couldn't be sure. Her brother had phoned during dinner to assure each family member that his flight to Philly was uneventful, and that he was home safe. But when he got to Amanda, Robby insisted in no uncertain terms that he speak to her privately and would call back at midnight.

What a drama king! She figured he'd lecture her, and she could easily turn down her ringer and avoid the call. On the other hand, she might as well get it over and done with. She got out of bed, put on her sneakers and a jacket, and quietly left her room.

As she passed through the hallway, she heard her mother and Trout softly talking in their bedroom. Thinking of them together and intimate gave her a queer feeling, just as imagining Ginny reading a bedtime story to her adorable little daughter Lissa made Amanda feel lonesome and alone. But as she tiptoed through the living room, Trout's old Doberman, Ursie, shuffled to her feet, nuzzled Amanda's hand and followed her outdoors to the porch.

She glanced up at the moon and zipped up her jacket as she and the dog jogged down to the gazebo on the dock. A chilly breeze whipped across the lake and waves slammed on the shore. Sitting down on the cold wooden bench, Amanda saw it was almost twelve and braced herself for the call. Ursie leaned her warm body against Amanda's leg and lay her long nose in her lap.

Her phone chirped right on cue, and she immediately picked up. "Okay, Robby, this better be good," she hissed.

In his typical lawyerly fashion, he beat around the bush with familial pleasantries, then cleared his throat for the summation. "Point is, Mandy, you're acting real pissy toward Mom, and it's not fair…"

When she tried to object, Robby overruled her and drowned her out. He dragged her all the way back to those horrific months after their parents' divorce and drove his point home:

"You never believed Mom when she told you the truth about Dad. Don't you remember how much he was drinking? He was abusive and dismissive of her, and yes, he was violent. He hit Mom."

"That's not true! Besides, how the hell would you know?"

For several long seconds, her brother was silent. When he spoke, his words were calm and measured. "I know because I saw it happen, and I saw Mom's bruises. I was older than you and I wanted to protect you. So did Mom."

"Since when?" Anger burned inside her, but suddenly she was insecure. It was so unlike her brother, the wuss, to be so adamant about anything.

"Did you hear me, Mandy? You just never saw that side of Dad. It's time you got over it and let all that hatred go."

"If he's such a monster, why do you work for him, Robby?"

He said quietly, "You know he's changed."

She did. Even as a runaway, Amanda had stayed in touch with her two best girlfriends. Over the years, they had gossiped about how Amanda's father had remarried and started a new family. In fact, Amanda had a half-brother she'd never even met. Her girlfriends had also said her dad now looked like an old man she'd hardly recognize.

"So what?" she asked her brother with less conviction.

"So, if you have any interest in that exhibit space Ginny described when I called before, you should seriously consider a short-term lease and repair your relationship with Mom before it's too late."

Amanda swallowed the lump in her throat and realized she was about to cry. "Look, I'll think about it, Robby," was all she could say.

"I'm glad to hear it," he said mildly, and then hung up.

She kept her composure for less than ten seconds, and then the tears began to flow. Who the hell did Robby think he was? Certainly he wasn't the brother she remembered. He had changed, but had she? Ten years of pent-up rage, or was it guilt, drained from her body. Ursie lifted her head, her liquid eyes filled with concern, and offered a little whine.

"It's okay, girl." Amanda rubbed the animal's folded velvet ears.

"You sure it's okay?" Suddenly Ginny appeared from nowhere. "I heard you leave the house. Is something wrong?"

Dressed in black jeans and a dark T-shirt, Ginny's only visible parts were her bare white feet. She had sneaked up like a ghost and scared Amanda witless.

Amanda tried to dry her eyes with the sleeve of her jacket. "Everything's fine."

Ginny slipped down beside her on the bench and touched her hand. "Who was that on the phone? Lovers' quarrel?"

"Hardly!" The very idea brought Amanda out of her funk and she barked with laughter.

"So what's up? Have you decided about Metrolina?"

Just then Ursie launched off Amanda's lap to chase a night creature lurking in the nearby bushes. The distraction gave Amanda time to think.

"Metrolina is a possibility," she told Ginny. "I just don't know how I'd manage it. The next show is only two weeks away, and all my finished work, supplies and equipment are down in Sarasota."

They both watched as Ursie flushed a great blue heron out of hiding. The magnificent bird squawked bloody murder, slow-walked on its clumsy, too long legs, and then beat its huge wings. It took flight just in time to avoid Ursie's snapping jaws.

"Well, that woke up the household," Amanda said as the Doberman kept barking.

"No kidding." Ginny laughed, and then she got serious. "So you need to get your stuff from Sarasota?"

Amanda nodded, her heart racing.

"No problem," Ginny answered quickly. "I'll borrow Trev's big van and we'll leave tomorrow. We'll go together!"

CHAPTER SIX

Ginny's story…

They took turns driving. As it turned out, Ginny did not borrow Trev's vehicle, because Amanda had a perfectly good, almost new Nissan NV200 Compact Cargo van waiting for her in Florida. And if she was going to do this thing, and there was no turning back now, she'd need to pack her meager possessions and sculpture supplies into her Nissan and move to North Carolina. Good God, how had that happened?

"I really don't mind helping with the gas money," Ginny said as Amanda topped off the tank in the red Ford Fiesta she had rented that morning at Avis in Mooresville. The plan was to drop it at the Avis in Sarasota when they were done, and then use the Nissan to drive home.

"I insist on paying for everything, Ginny, including the motels. After all, you didn't really need to come. I could have managed this trip by myself." Amanda glanced at her stepsister, who seemed unhappy with the financial arrangements. "But I really appreciate your company," she hastened to add, even though it was a lie.

They had left at the crack of dawn. Amanda's mom, Trout and even little Lissa had crawled out of bed to see them off. Everyone, especially her mother, seemed shell-shocked by Amanda's sudden decision to give North Carolina a try. Indeed, Amanda could tell that her mom was giddy with joy but deliberately held her emotions in check. She seemed to fear that any show of gushiness would kill the deal. Amanda had emphasized the move was a trial run, that she intended to sign up for only a three-month lease. Everything, including her newfound family, was on probation. But nothing dampened their enthusiasm. Trout served pancakes and sausages while Lissa, on a maple syrup high, jumped up and down shouting, "Road trip! Road trip!"

Naturally, the seven-year-old wanted to come. She was no dummy, she knew Disney World was on their route. At that point, Amanda again tried to discourage Ginny from tagging along, but Ginny had insisted she needed a break from her job at Buffalo Guys, from wedding planning, even from Trev. It seemed the groom was becoming anxious as the big day approached. Besides, Ginny reasoned, Amanda needed help with all her heavy stuff.

"Lissa's gonna love staying with her grandparents a couple of days," Ginny said as they got back on the road. "Dad and Diana spoil her rotten."

Amanda nodded absently, her eyes glued to the highway, her hands tense on the wheel. They had stopped at Metrolina early that morning so Amanda could sign the lease and get her pass and key. Then they had immediately crossed into South Carolina and were already in north Georgia, where Ginny started jabbering about peaches. According to Google Maps, the entire trip would take nine hours and forty-three minutes, six hundred sixty-four miles, without stops or traffic disruptions. Amanda calculated they had at least six more hours to go.

"When I was younger, a trip like this was no big deal," Amanda said. "But maybe we should split it up, stop somewhere for the night." Her stomach was growling and she was fighting a headache. She had stupidly left her sunglasses at the lake home.

"Yeah, I know what you mean," Ginny agreed. "I once drove all the way to Vegas in two days, hardly stopped to eat or pee."

"But we're getting older, right?" As much as Amanda dreaded spending a night in a motel with Ginny, with all the personal conversation that would require, she dreaded their arrival in Sarasota even more. Her life there was private, a carefully guarded secret from most of the world, especially her family. Clearly she had not thought this through.

"Speak for yourself, Mandy," Ginny said. "*I'm* not getting old, so let's keep moving. Besides, I hate you paying for a motel."

"Well, I plan to treat you to a really nice hotel when we get there," Amanda said.

"Really? Why can't we stay at your place?"

Amanda felt like she'd been punched in the gut. It was a fair question, but staying at her former residence was not an option. "It's complicated," she answered carefully, giving Ginny a warning look.

She could almost hear her stepsister's mind working, but to her credit, Ginny kept her mouth shut and did not ask. This was one of the many things she'd quickly learned to love about Ginny—she did not pry. Maybe because she had baggage of her own, she respected Amanda's space.

"Let's stop for lunch though," Amanda suggested. "There's a McDonald's at the next exit, and I'd kill for a quarter pounder with cheese."

"Agreed."

Amanda bought a cheap pair of sunglasses and some Tylenol at a drugstore beside the restaurant, and then Ginny drove the next stint. As Amanda watched the changing landscape, she was thankful to listen to Ginny finally opening up about her own rebellious past. She did this in fits and starts, like a jerky download on a slow computer. Amanda learned that Ginny had been secretly pregnant with Lissa when she ran away from home. Even the father, Trev Dula, did not know he had fathered a child.

Ginny had landed in Galveston, Texas. She immediately married an oil man named Charley Harkin, hoping to give her unborn child a daddy with income. Charley, who was ten years older than Ginny, accepted Lissa just fine, even loved both mother and child—until Hurricane Katrina wiped out his job and life as he'd known it. After that, Ginny's marriage rapidly disintegrated, and she divorced the abusive, alcoholic man Charley had become.

The story made Amanda's head spin. "I am so sorry!" she told Ginny.

"Yeah, it was a shitty situation, but in the end it worked out. It got me off my butt and out of that Texas hellhole. I moved to Las Vegas and started a new life…"

Amanda closed her eyes as Ginny explained how she'd named her daughter after Melissa Etheridge, the lesbian rock n' roll icon. Amanda took this as a good sign that her stepsister was at least open-minded. Then Ginny described how some old lady had taken her under her wing and provided shelter in Vegas during Ginny's lean years as a cocktail waitress. Eventually she got a job as a croupier, earning substantial tips that allowed her to rent a nice apartment.

"So why did you leave such a glamorous life to return to North Carolina?" Amanda asked sleepily.

"I had to. Trevor Dula, the love of my life, was about to marry someone else. I couldn't allow that to happen, could I?" she finished with a wicked grin.

"So fate brought you and Trev back together?" Amanda asked.

"That's right, with a lot of help from your mom."

Amanda didn't want to know. She was sick and tired of everyone singing her mother's praises. "Why don't you pull over and let me drive the last leg?"

She was relieved when Ginny curled up, her dark head cushioned between the headrest and the window, and went sound asleep. It gave Amanda breathing room to digest Ginny's story, as well as organize her own thoughts.

The sun was beginning a leisurely descent in the western sky as they neared the Tampa Bay Bridge. During the long day they had passed through hills, lowlands, lake country, farmland and cities. They had seen poor double-wide trailers and multimillion dollar mansions. The foliage had shifted from Carolina hardwoods and Georgia pines to Florida palms and live oaks. The atmosphere had gone from fresh clear morning to tropical humidity. And Amanda's personal thermostat was also on the rise as she worried about Ginny's reaction to *her* story, which was bound to be partially revealed when they reached their destination.

"Wake up, Ginny. I need to ask you a question."

"Where are we?" She rubbed her eyes, smearing the mascara she always wore, and then gazed in wonder at the blinding, aqua water flowing under the mighty bridge. "Shit, why didn't you wake me sooner? This is amazing!"

"Remember last night when Ursie almost got that blue heron?" Amanda asked. "What would have happened if she had caught it?"

Ginny blinked like Amanda was crazy. After all, last night seemed very far away. "What do you mean?"

"Would Ursie have killed it?"

Ginny's right cheek was creased from sleep as she carefully considered her answer. "I don't know. It's a game they've played for years. Ursie pretends to hate the heron, acts like she wants to tear it to shreds. And the bird is scared to death of her. But if Ursie actually connected and hurt it, I think it would break both their hearts."

CHAPTER SEVEN

Towles Court...

"This is paradise, Mandy! Why the fuck would you ever leave this place?"

During the hour since they'd crossed the Tampa Bay Bridge, Ginny's enthusiasm for Florida had ramped up in decibels, the volume of *ooh's* and *ah's* so loud Amanda longed for a switch to turn her down.

"I have no idea why the fuck I'm leaving." It was a lie. Of course Amanda knew. Her situation in Sarasota had become unbearable.

Amanda had deliberately chosen the scenic route, avoiding the seedier parts of town. Currently they were on US 41, cruising past the causeway that led out to wealthy Longboat Key, with the Gulf of Mexico ahead and Sarasota Bay behind. They circled around the famous twenty-six foot tall sculpture of the sailor kissing a nurse, which soared above the park and yacht club.

"It's called *Unconditional Surrender*, a serviceman coming home after World War II," Amanda explained. "The cultural snoots in town want to get rid of it. They think it's an eyesore."

"I think it's hot," Ginny said as her head swiveled from one side of the street to the other. "Check out those high rise condos. It must cost a fortune to live here."

True. For the most part, this was a rich man's town, which was one reason Amanda had been able to survive by selling her funky metal sculpture.

"Where's your gallery? Can we drive by it before checking into the hotel?" Ginny asked.

Amanda had revealed the bare minimum about her personal living situation. Ginny did know that Amanda was part of an arts community and that she shared a home, which was attached to their retail space, with another woman, who was a painter.

"Okay, we'll drive past the gallery. It's not too far from here." But Amanda had no intention of stopping in, not tonight.

As she navigated the heavy tourist traffic, not to mention the locals coming out for the nightlife, Amanda steered west of route 301 and turned onto Adams Lane.

"This is it, Towles Court Artist Colony." She pulled to the curb at the periphery of a quaint, heavily treed compound consisting of several blocks of classic Florida bungalows. These were occupied by two dozen artists—photographers to jewelry craftsmen.

Her heart was beating double-time and her hands were sweating on the steering wheel. Amanda fervently hoped no one she knew was out and about at this in-between time—after the shops closed but before the dinner rush. Having lived in this small community for seven years, she knew all the residents, and fortunately they all seemed to be inside their houses.

Unfortunately, Amanda's house was directly outside Ginny's car window. Amanda's partner, Rachel Lessing, had purchased the charming bungalow. Painted turquoise blue with a bright red door, it had a little garden surrounded by a white picket fence, both shaded by the branches of two enormous oaks. Rachel had chosen it precisely because the building was so visible and attracted foot traffic.

Ginny caught on immediately. "This is it, isn't it? The sign says *Luna Studios*, just like you said. Oh, it's so cute, Mandy. Can't we go in now, just for a minute?"

"Absolutely not." Amanda saw the nose of her white Nissan poking out from under the carport, but saw no sign of Rachel's BMW. She shifted into drive, prepared to make a quick retreat, when all of a sudden the red studio door swung open and two women stepped out.

"Oh shit!" Amanda groaned and sank low in her seat. Rachel would not recognize their red rental car, nor did she know Ginny, so they had a good shot at remaining anonymous.

"Look, someone's home, Mandy. Can't we go in?"

"No! Please be quiet, and don't say one word to them."

"Why not? You'll have to let them know we're coming tomorrow because we have to pick up your stuff."

"I realize that," Amanda hissed. "I'll call her tonight. I just don't want to see her now." She sank even lower as the pair strolled arm in arm down the pathway, toward the street.

"Which one's Rachel?" Ginny persisted.

"Shut up, damn it!"

As they came closer, laughing and completely engrossed in one another, Amanda's chest constricted. Rachel's long, curly dark hair was pulled back in a loose ponytail, and even at that distance Amanda saw the endearing strands of gray at her temples while her intelligent, intense brown eyes were riveted to the much younger woman at her side. The other woman—small, blond, perky as hell—had been one of Rachel's students, just as Amanda had been. She knew the girl's name was Candace, but Rachel called her Candy. Amanda hated Candy with all her heart and soul.

"Rachel's the one on the left?" Ginny whispered.

"Yeah, that's right." Amanda realized Ginny was staring at her.

"So who's the other woman?"

"Someone who went to the head of the class," Amanda answered bitterly.

"Oh, I see."

Amanda turned her head away as the couple passed not ten feet from the car. Once they were safely down the street, she squeezed back the tears threatening to leak out. She watched them round the corner, where Rachel's BMW was parked.

Ginny took her hand and held on hard. The gesture made her agony worse.

"Mandy, look at me."

"What do you want?" Amanda reluctantly faced her.

"I get it," Ginny said softly. "Rachel Lessing is much more than a friend, isn't she?"

CHAPTER EIGHT

Lavender Blue...

What could she say? Clearly Ginny knew the ways of the world, so if Amanda denied her relationship with Rachel, Ginny would know she was lying. So she said nothing.

"God, I really am sorry," Ginny said. "How long were you guys together?"

Rachel's BMW drove away and out of sight.

"Maybe it was the seven-year itch?" Amanda said. "Diana says real estate clients change houses every seven years, like in that old Marilyn Monroe movie where men tire of their wives every seven years? I think Rachel just wanted to trade in for a newer model."

"Then Rachel's crazy. That skanky little girl's got nothing on you, Mandy."

"Thanks for the vote of confidence, but I really don't want to talk about it." In fact, she doubted she could speak at all. Her mouth was dry and her heart was pounding. She had dreaded this moment forever, being outed to a family member. But instead of the devastating bang she'd expected, Ginny's reaction was more like a whimper.

"So is the bitch living with Rachel now?"

"Yes, she is." Candy had usurped Amanda's bedroom, the kitchen where she had done all the cooking, even her work studio. Insult to injury, Amanda's replacement wasn't even a serious artist. Candy painted watercolor greeting cards with talking-head flowers spewing little clichés of wisdom extolling the sweetness of life. Amanda couldn't imagine what Rachel saw in her.

"So she just threw you out?"

"Look, Ginny, I didn't have a say in the matter. Rachel owns the house, and it's not like we were married or anything." Of course, Amanda had felt married, but she had no legal claim to anything. A whole chunk of her life had been wasted, leaving only a dark hole where it once had been.

"Bummer," Ginny said.

Amanda drove wordlessly toward a famous bed-and-breakfast she'd heard about. Although no one she knew had actually forked out the cash to stay there, she wanted to give Ginny a special treat, to thank her for helping with this difficult move. When Amanda pulled up outside the two-storied wooden Victorian, like something right out of a Hemingway novel, Ginny's eyes lit up in wonder.

"Stay in the car until I check in," Amanda said. "I'll be right back."

And she was right back, crestfallen.

"What's wrong?" Ginny's face fell.

"I should have made a reservation. I am a very stupid woman." Amanda smacked her forehead. "I'm really sorry, but I'm sure we'll find someplace else."

But as Amanda ticked off their options, she soon realized that without a reservation they'd have to settle for one of the cheap motels on South Tamiami. A Google search located a Super 8 not far from the Avis where they would drop the Fiesta. She called and reserved two nights.

"I apologize, Ginny. This wasn't what I wanted, but I'll make it up to you by treating you to a great dinner."

"No problem."

They were only a few blocks away from what used to be Amanda and Rachel's favorite restaurant. Since their habit had been to eat there during the Third Friday Gallery Walks, Amanda was pretty sure the pattern would hold and they wouldn't run into her ex on this Tuesday night. Besides, she'd already seen the happy couple leave the neighborhood, so she drove back to Adams Lane and parked at Lavender Blue.

"Am I dressed okay for a place like this?" Ginny's eyes widened as they approached the restaurant built in a green oasis, definitely a romantic setting.

"You look great." In fact, they were both rumpled and wilted from almost twelve hours on the road. She ran her fingers through her hair and smoothed out her khakis, yet she knew the folks who owned this restaurant—not to mention the patrons, many of whom would know her—had seen her far less presentable. As for Ginny, with her long tan legs extending from cut-off jean shorts, her low-cut string blouse showing plenty of voluptuous cleavage, her black punk cut and nose stud—she'd fit right in.

"The couple who owns this place have been like parents to me," she told Ginny as the hostess took them straight to a special table outside on the wraparound porch. "We don't need reservations here."

"Everyone's staring at us," Ginny whispered, sounding self-conscious.

"No, they're staring at *me*. They all thought I'd left town." Suddenly Amanda feared she'd made a terrible mistake coming here. As many heads swiveled in her direction, she recognized fellow artists from the community and two past clients. By now, everyone would have heard the story of her dramatic breakup—Rachel's version—and as they were seated, some people looked away, embarrassed at having caught her eye.

"So are you okay with this?" Ginny wondered.

"Sure, it's no big deal."

But it was. One thing Amanda knew for certain was that within the hour, Rachel would know she was in town. She needed to phone her ex and explain the visit before she heard God knew what from someone else.

A waiter arrived with co-owner Petra right behind him. He handed them menus and stepped aside so that Petra could pour Amanda's favorite wine.

"You are back, darling!" she said to Amanda in a unique accent that was hard to pin down.

"Only a visit. We leave again day after tomorrow."

"Oh, I am so sorry to hear this." She gave Ginny a curious glance, so Amanda introduced her. "I hope you both will enjoy the dinner, and this wine is on the house. Once Ivan hears who he is cooking for, he will make it very special."

"Thanks, Petra," Amanda said, and when they left, she choked back a bittersweet emotion she couldn't quite define.

Ginny took it all in, especially the elegant menu. "Everything's so expensive. Are you sure about this, Mandy?"

Amanda smiled. "Absolutely. By the way, Petra and Ivan are Croatian. He trained as a chef in Sarajevo, during the famous Winter Olympics."

Her stepsister nodded, seeming somewhat overwhelmed. Yet Ginny had experienced fine dining and an exotic, international atmosphere in Las Vegas, so Amanda figured either she was tired from the trip, or something else was going on. Once they had ordered, Amanda excused herself to make the dreaded phone call to Rachel.

By the time she returned to the porch, feeling bruised and abused by her ex's icy displeasure at hearing her voice, not to mention Rachel's hot anger that Amanda would be disrupting her plans for the following day, she saw Ginny flirting with the waiter. And the food was on the table.

"How did it go?" Ginny asked once the waiter had left and Amanda was seated.

"It was like walking barefoot on dry ice, or maybe red hot coals."

"Sounds like fun."

They dug into the food. Ginny had ordered the sea scallops with toasted almonds, amoretto and cream. Amanda had a classic ribeye crusted with black peppercorns and sautéed mushrooms, served with brandy flambé cream sauce. She hoped the red meat would boost her energy for what lay ahead. But it was the wine that really helped. It went straight to her head, numbing the many little needles of apprehension prickling her flesh. The alcohol affected Ginny too. She couldn't stop giggling.

"What's so funny?" Amanda asked once Ivan himself had served their coffee.

"Did you see how Ivan looked at us?" Ginny giggled even harder. "Don't you get it, Mandy? Everyone thinks I'm your new best thang. They think we're together!"

Amanda was stunned. "You mean like *together* together? No way."

"Why not?" Ginny batted her mascaraed eyelashes. "You think I'm hot, right?"

Amanda almost choked on her coffee. Clearly her crazy stepsister was drunk. "That's absolutely ridiculous, Ginny. Lower your voice."

"Ridiculous? Really?" Ginny leaned closer across the tablecloth, candlelight glittering in her teasing dark eyes. "When I was in Vegas I experimented a little, you know? Especially after my jerk husband Charley. And I gotta say, women get it right."

Surely Amanda had misheard, or misunderstood, or just plain missed it concerning her straight-as-an-arrow hetero stepsister. "What about Trevor?" she gasped.

Ginny rolled her eyes up at the tropical fan lazily spinning near the porch ceiling. "That's just it. When Trev miraculously came back into the realm of possibility, I left them all behind— all the sweet boys, and girls."

"Jesus, Ginny!" Amanda felt foolish, naïve, but mostly disoriented when Ginny reached under the table and squeezed her hand. While she usually considered herself worldly, a fair judge of human nature, life often intervened and gave her a swift kick in the backside. She quickly pulled her hand away and hid it in her lap.

"You know what else, Mandy?" Ginny winked.

Amanda held her breath. Did she really want to know?

"All these friends of yours in this restaurant…? I just played along. Now they *really* think we're lovers."

"What did you say, Ginny?" Amanda couldn't take one more shock that evening.

"Doesn't matter." Ginny yawned. "But I'll tell you one thing, I'm about to drop dead. Can we go to the motel now?"

"Yeah, I guess so," Amanda answered wryly. "If you promise not to jump my bones during the night."

CHAPTER NINE

Some vulnerable soft tissue…

After a deep night's sleep, free of hanky-panky of any kind, Ginny woke up fresh and gung-ho for the moving adventure ahead. After the evening's gastronomic excesses, they had settled for the motel's puny breakfast of stale croissants and overripe fruit. After her third cup of weak coffee, Amanda figured she too was ready to start the day. In spite of the terrible nightmare she'd had that destroyed her rest big-time.

It featured a ghostly cast of actors who did and did not resemble people in her real life. Women vaguely resembling Diana, Ginny and Liz had struggled upstream on a raft. The odd waterway, a menacing hybrid of alligator infested wetlands and Lake Norman, was rushing backward toward a precipitous drop over the dam at the nuclear station. The men—Trout, Trevor and Danny—tried to help from the shore, but as they chopped at trees, rang school bells and cast ropes at the river, nothing worked.

Eventually they all converged at a decaying southern mansion with holes in the floors and desperate birds dive-bombing the windows. An emaciated version of Rachel, leading a pet that was half dog, half Candy, floated through the dark hallways singing off-key. At the bottom of the grand rotting staircase, reflected in a tall, ornate mirror, Amanda saw the chiaroscuro images of Sara and Marc, the sister and brother from Metrolina, smiling and waving, as from a great distance.

"Did you sleep well?" Ginny popped a soggy strawberry into her mouth.

"Not really. I had a bad dream."

"Wanna talk about it?"

"Not really."

"Okay, so what did it mean? You should take dreams seriously. I do," Ginny said.

"I don't." Amanda grabbed her purse, took out her car key, and moved toward the door.

The artist colony was still asleep when they pulled up at Towles Court. At least, Amanda hoped it was, because if they could get in and out quickly, without speaking to a single solitary soul, it was okay with her. She marched straight to her Nissan van, which was parked in the dappled shade of the carport, with Ginny following hot on her tail.

"Shouldn't we let them know we're here?"

"Nope. They'll know soon enough." She opened the two rear doors, and the familiar smell of steel and Rustoleum paint wafted out. The big white van had been used exclusively for transporting her sculpture and materials, while she and Rachel had used the BMW for their social life.

"Nice ride, it's almost new," Ginny commented. "Must have cost you a pretty penny. What's her name?"

Amanda hesitated.

"You do name your cars, don't you?"

Amanda blushed. "I call her Moby most of the time, but she's Moby Dyke to our closer circle of friends."

Ginny guffawed. "I love it!"

Amanda held a finger to her lips. "Can you please keep quiet?" She pulled out a pile of loading blankets and tossed them at Ginny. "We'll pack the big stuff first, then go to my studio for the finished pieces."

She led her helper to a rickety wooden lean-to adjacent to the carport, then opened its door to a dusty space filled with cobwebs. When she pulled the string to the overhead light, Ginny gasped.

"Holy shit, look at all this!" She wandered into the chaos and touched Amanda's big flower, a six foot tall tangle of welded tailpipes topped with giant gear blossoms. The stems were sprayed green, the gears bright yellow, and the whole arrangement was anchored in a ten-gallon steel bucket.

"I call that one *Sunflowers*," Amanda said.

"What about this?" Ginny flopped into a chair with tailpipe legs and a wraparound back fashioned from the organic chrome bumpers of a vintage Cadillac. Amanda had made the cushions of black crushed velvet.

"That's Wing chair and that's Cock Table." Amanda pointed at the matching side table, which also had twisted tailpipe legs and an antique steering wheel set horizontally beneath a round plate glass to hold the cocktails.

"Fucking awesome!" Ginny shouted. "I want everything!"

Several other pieces of pop art furniture, including a couch and floor lamps, filled the room—along with the rusty raw materials Amanda used to make them.

"I hope you have lots of auto graveyards in North Carolina," Amanda said.

"Are you kidding? Auto parts are what we do best. You'll think you've died and gone to heaven, Mandy."

"Good thing, because we can't take everything."

"Well, we have to bring the flowers and furniture," Ginny insisted.

As Amanda gazed at her life's work, it hurt to accept that she'd have to leave some art behind. They could fit a few special pieces into the van, and maybe the cardboard art tubes filled with the precious rods she used to solder the welds, but all the carefully scavenged bits of scrap would have to be sacrificed. She explained this to Ginny, along with the order in which the items would be packed, and then they got started.

They were carrying the heavy Wing Chair when Ginny offered a bizarre idea:

"When you called Rachel last night, did you tell her I was your stepsister?"

"No..." Amanda answered cautiously. "Why?"

"Because why should you? Why can't we let her assume I'm your lover, just like they did last night at the restaurant?"

Amanda almost dropped her end of the load. "You are absolutely insane!"

"No, why not? Rachel deserves it, and it would be kick-ass fun, Mandy."

Ginny's whispered suggestion was sly, evil, and completely delicious. It appealed to the dark gods of pure revenge. "I suppose it wouldn't hurt if Rachel jumped to the wrong conclusion..." Amanda could almost taste the sweet justice on her lips.

At the same time, just as they'd made their pact with the devil, a dark shadow blocked the doorway. The apparition looked much like the emaciated ghost from Amanda's nightmare.

"Hello Amanda." Rachel's deep voice echoed in the storage room.

"Hello Rach." But Amanda saw that her ex was not looking at her; but rather she was glaring at Ginny.

Ginny put down her end of the chair. "Hi, I'm Ginny Troutman, Amanda's friend." She held out her hand for Rachel to shake.

Amanda noticed that Ginny had attached just the right innuendo to the word *friend*, and by the way Rachel refused Ginny's hand, Amanda knew her ex had taken the bait. Glory hallelujah, the games were on.

"I've never heard anything about you," Rachel said.

Ginny shrugged. "No problem, because I've heard a lot about you."

Amanda realized the temperature in the crowded space had gone up about twenty degrees. "Look, Rach, we don't want to disturb your routine, so why don't you go back to the house. Ginny and I will finish up here, and then we'll join you."

After a long, inscrutable look—something between panic and regret—Rachel agreed to leave. She took the time to glance back over her shoulder and smile at Amanda. More than anything so far, that smile wounded Amanda in some vulnerable soft tissue she'd thought was already dead.

"Well, that went well," Ginny said before they got back to work.

"Not exactly." Something about this deception was stirring pangs of guilt, and it wasn't fair that she should feel this way. "Let's get this done, then get the hell outta here."

Forty-five minutes later, sweaty and aching from the contortions of jigsaw-puzzling the oddly angled sculpture into the van, with little room left for more, they entered Luna Studios and went directly to Amanda's sunny room at the front of the building. She'd already told Ginny how she had done all her welding outside, on a sheltered patio at the back of the property. She hadn't wanted to burn the house down, after all. She had used this inside studio for assembling the small mobiles and tabletop pieces, which were Amanda's financial bread and butter. Some she spray-painted, others she burnished so the different materials—aluminum, copper or steel—were featured in their natural beauty.

"I hope these will sell at Metrolina. They pay the grocery bills."

"They will," Ginny assured her.

When Amanda opened the door to her room, assuming they'd be alone, she was startled to see a young woman sitting at her desk.

Candy glanced up from her project. If looks could kill, Amanda and Ginny were dead meat.

"I suppose you want me to leave?" Candy tossed her shoulder-length blond hair and pinned them with her strange green cat eyes. She was painting her greeting cards in an assembly line, adding flower heads to them all, and then the verses.

"Pretty pictures," Ginny snidely observed.

"They pay the grocery bills," Candy coldly replied, echoing what Amanda had just said.

Amanda laughed out loud. In the end, whether an artist considered her work fine or funk, they all had the same goal: to survive in a business where it was almost impossible to make a living. As she threaded her way across the cluttered floor, with Candy's boxes of paper and pots of paint scattered underfoot, she felt an unwelcome sympathy for the girl—until she opened her closet.

Someone, obviously Candy, because Rachel would not do such a thing, had thrown all of Amanda's delicate mobiles together in a box. The resulting jumble of tangled wire parts would take hours to unwind. Amanda's stock of small sculpture was carelessly tossed, one upon another, in a pile in the corner. Fortunately, they were more or less indestructible.

Determined to control her temper, Amanda bit her tongue, then said, "I will need about twelve boxes and some Bubble Wrap."

"We don't have that stuff here." Candy rolled her shoulders and stretched.

"Well, then. Maybe you girls should go out and buy some." As before, Rachel Lessing had magically appeared in the doorway. This time, however, she was neither emaciated nor ghost-like, but rather a substantial force of nature. "Candy, you know that storage unit place near the hardware? They have packing materials there. Ginny, you go with her to help. Take my credit card."

Candy was huffy and affronted, while Ginny looked to Amanda for rescue, which never came. Amanda knew better than to contradict Rachel in one of her moods, so as her ex-lover handed Candy the car keys and what Amanda assumed was a fully loaded Visa, she nodded to Ginny to play along.

"Take the BMW. The supplies will fit in the trunk," Rachel instructed. "And take your time, will you? Amanda and I need about an hour alone."

CHAPTER TEN

Everything had changed...

Once the women left, stomping off together in unspoken protest, Amanda hoped they would arrive at a truce during their outing. And she especially hoped she would survive the next sixty minutes with Rachel. But for now, they simply watched one another.

For the first time, Amanda noticed that Rachel had aged dramatically. More strands of gray were visible in her unruly mane of black hair and webs of worry lines radiated from the corners of her eyes and mouth. Those dark, intensely intelligent eyes were underhung with the palest of blue circles. They had been apart only a little over a month, so either this change had happened very fast, or else Amanda hadn't been paying attention. She suspected the latter. Maybe they had not really *seen* one another for a very long time.

But after all, Rachel was ten years older, and hadn't that been part of the attraction? She was the wise one—mentor, teacher, best friend. Aside from Maya Colgan in high school, Rachel had been Amanda's only lover, teaching her everything she hoped to know about intimacy. So what the hell happened? And what did Rachel see now, as they stared at one another?

"So, how are you?" Amanda began.

"Hanging in." Rachel rocked her hand side to side, in a familiar gesture meaning neither here nor there. "Do you want a cup of tea?"

So this was how it was going to be: act normal, like nothing had ever happened between them. The absurdity took her breath away as she followed Rachel to the kitchen. Here too everything had changed.

The room was a pigsty, with dirty dishes in the sink and covering the countertops. When Rachel opened the fridge, Amanda saw wilted lettuce, cartons of Chinese takeout, a gummy ketchup bottle, and precious little else. She, who had kept the kitchen spotless and cooked a thousand gourmet meals, was astounded.

"Candy's not much of a housekeeper," Rachel conceded as she set the kettle on the stove. "But that's okay. We eat out most nights."

Amanda felt a growing unease as Rachel went about the simple domestic ceremony they had shared each day. She dunked the teabags into the mugs they always used, souvenirs from the Everglades, while she hummed "You Are My Sunshine," as she always did during this ritual.

Amanda was so unnerved she began to babble incessantly. In a great rush of words, she told Rachel all about her trip to North Carolina to attend her mother's wedding, about her reunion with her brother Robby, and her fondness for Trout. All this had happened since they parted, so Rachel knew none of it.

Rachel stopped humming and listened attentively. All the while, she watched Amanda with those eyes.

"But you hate your mother," she said when Amanda paused.

A stream of sunlight angled through the café curtains and danced on the table as it always had. The curtains were still patterned with seashells, but everything else had changed.

"I was wrong," Amanda answered slowly, surprising herself. "Maybe I made a mistake about my mother."

"Really?" Rachel's comment dripped sarcasm, disbelief.

And why wouldn't she feel that way? Rachel had endured seven years of Amanda's complaints against her mother. The ceramic wall clock, shaped like a sea turtle, ticked into the long silence as it always had, but Amanda sensed an elemental shift had taken place. She no longer felt crippling anger toward her mother, but she couldn't think about that right now.

"Well, I've made mistakes too," Rachel admitted. "Especially lately..." She fixed Amanda with a look imparting some great truth.

But what was the takeaway? What was Amanda to glean from this confession? She would not, could not, think about it.

"Come, I want to show you something." Suddenly Rachel was on her feet, striding toward the large studio at the back of the house where she painted. "I really want your honest opinion, Amanda."

When they rounded the corner, and Rachel stepped aside, Amanda was dumbfounded by the transformation of the room. Rachel had cleared away all the clutter, and most of the finished pieces Amanda had seen previously were missing. She had stripped the shades from the windows and painted the scuffed walls pale yellow. New small oil paintings were stacked neatly against the walls. But the enormous canvas on the easel, which dominated the room with its sheer power, took Amanda's breath away.

Yes, it was a landscape, but Rachel had always done landscapes. Now her style was totally different. Instead of the gentle, somewhat Impressionist studies she was known for, this piece had distilled the very essence of land, river and sky into a shimmering abstraction of the marshland—a study in lights and darks that captured a strong current moving under the deceptively lazy river. Amanda felt the tall grasses moving under the active clouds and smelled the primal organisms in the mud along the riverbank. Rachel had accomplished this with a few carefully placed washes of color: pale coral to vibrant orange and rust, soft blue to hidden cobalt. The end product was a visceral punch to the gut. It was bold, beautiful and scary.

It was, in fact, the scene from Amanda's nightmare, when she'd been struggling upstream on the raft, desperate to reach shore. She could almost see the decaying southern mansion over the horizon, where frantic birds beat against the windows.

Only now, in the bright light of day, Rachel's painting was not a fearsome thing. It was a nurturing dream, pulling Amanda into its womb-like warmth.

"Well?" Rachel crossed her arms and stood to one side.

"God, Rach, I don't know what to say. It's amazing, magnificent. What has happened to you?" One thing Amanda knew with certainty: the mysterious "mistakes" Rachel had made lately had nothing to do with her painting.

"I don't know what happened," her ex admitted. "When we broke up, I threw things away. I sold all my old work and started fresh."

Rachel's talent had always been enormous, but now she had ramped it up far more than several notches. Art dealers would be tearing down her door just to get their hands on this work.

"Congratulations," Amanda said with feeling. For once she wasn't even jealous of her mentor; she was overwhelmed with pride. "Is Candy your new inspiration?" She had to ask.

Rachel shrugged. "Is Ginny yours?"

Suddenly Amanda was ashamed of the deception. "Look, Rach, Ginny isn't my girlfriend, she's my stepsister."

Rachel's eyebrows arched in surprise. Amanda wished she could read more into her former lover's expression—like maybe Rachel was relieved that Amanda had not moved on—but as always, the look was inscrutable.

"Since when do you have a stepsister?"

"Long story." Amanda sighed, unwilling to elaborate.

"Well, I'm happy for you," Rachel said and opened her arms.

Amanda froze. Should she take those half dozen steps back into Rachel's embrace? Clearly a business-like handshake was the smarter option, but then, Amanda had never been that smart. She crossed the room.

Suddenly they were holding one another. Amanda felt Rachel's breasts against hers, the beating of her heart, the woman's strong hands on her back. She also felt Rachel's tears on her cheeks and understood they were on the edge of an emotional volcano.

"I'm going to miss you, Amanda."

"I miss you already, Rach."

They stopped short of a kiss, and for a long moment, held one another at arm's length to say good-bye.

When Amanda heard the BMW pull up in the driveway, the sound of slamming car doors, she broke loose, smiled, and with all the dignity she could muster, she turned her back and walked away.

In a perfect world, that would have been the grand finale. But there was still work to be done, so Amanda dried her tears and listened as Ginny and Candy struggled into the house with the boxes and rolls of Bubble Wrap. Amazingly, they were laughing together like best pals.

Rachel remained sequestered in her studio while the three of them finished packing and loading. Amanda had taken all her personal items, clothes and whatnot, when she originally left. At least they didn't have to deal with those. It was determined that Amanda would leave her acetylene welding tanks behind, as the gas was far too unstable to transport them. She explained to Candy that the tanks were leased, and if she would be so kind as to return them to the company, they would refund Amanda her security deposit. She gave Candy her address at Trout's lake home in North Carolina so she could receive the check.

She retrieved her precious case of welding wands, her safety mask, and blessedly soon they were ready to go—the perfect anticlimax to a highly dramatic day.

"Are you okay, Mandy?" Ginny asked as they walked to the van.

"Yeah, I think I am." She glanced back at the window of Rachel's studio and thought she saw Rachel watching from the shadows. "I'm ready to move on."

CHAPTER ELEVEN

Horseplay…

Once they got home to North Carolina, she and Ginny slept for one solid day. They had both been hysterical with exhaustion by the time their heads hit the pillows, and Amanda slept the deep dreamless sleep of the dead. Her only visitor was Ursie, who tried to wake her up by pressing her cold doggie nose against her cheek and giving her a big sloppy kiss. It didn't work.

Ginny's sleep, on the other hand, had been rudely interrupted by Lissa jumping on her bed. Her pent-up daughter would not take no for an answer. She pestered Ginny until her mom climbed yawning from her nest and presented Lissa with the Mickey Mouse ears they'd bought the kid at a tourist rest stop miles from Disney World.

When Amanda finally emerged, she was shocked to discover it was Saturday. The lost week would eventually fade from memory, she supposed, but in the meantime, it was high time she rejoined the world.

"Have some more grits, Mandy." Trout passed the bowl and loaded her plate with more bacon, eggs and toast. That was great, because Amanda was ravenously hungry.

"Eat up, because you'll need all the energy you can get today," Ginny added as she slurped her orange juice.

"Why, what's happening?"

Her mother laughed. "Your big van is blocking us all in, so it's time you got your cute little fanny down to Metrolina and unpacked."

Amanda blinked at Ginny. "We're unpacking today?"

"Not me, I've already done my bit. Trev and Danny have volunteered to help. You could use some male muscle on the job."

Obviously the day had been planned for her. Diana and Liz were wildly busy with real estate now that the Great Recession was receding. Trout, who owned a convenience store/auto repair shop/gas station on River Highway, had been playing grandpa for three days and had to get back to work. Amanda knew her stepdad was semiretired and no longer needed to put in the long hours. But she also knew Trout loved to jaw with the customers and got antsy when his gossip line was severed.

"And Trev says it's my turn to hold down the fort at Buffalo Guys," Ginny added. "I must catch up with the bookwork, and since it's Saturday, I'll be onstage tonight."

Ginny, in addition to being the restaurant's accountant, was also its feature attraction. She played guitar and sang, and she was damned good, Amanda had heard.

"Do I have any say in this?" Amanda asked.

"No!" they all said in unison.

"But who's going to watch Lissa?"

"Don't worry, Aunt Mandy," she piped up. "I'm going to a picnic and sleepover at my girlfriend's house."

* * *

She felt more than a little silly squeezed into Moby's front seat with two large men she hardly knew. Trev was an ex-marine, with the physique and bravado that implied. His tan hairy leg in cut-off jeans pressed against her thigh as she drove.

Liz's Danny, with his curly brown hair, long gangly limbs and jovial nature, was a building contractor with a fresh joke for every mile. The boys knew each other well, kept jabbing one another with their elbows, distracting her. Indeed the handsome pair would turn heads at Metrolina, possibly even promote Amanda's image as a straight woman—but what was this, high school?

"Will you guys knock it off? You're going to cause an accident."

But her plea only heightened the horseplay, so when they arrived safely at Building 16, Amanda was the first one out of the van. The north entrance was already open and the three of them barreled inside, where Amanda pointed to Space D to their left. "That's my booth over there."

"Awesome!" Danny whistled. "It's a lot bigger than I expected."

"Yeah, but it sure needs a coat of paint," Trev pointed out. "And won't you need some display shelves?"

"What about lights? It's kind of dark in here."

They were right. Space D was more battered than she remembered. "I see what you mean. So let's start by unloading my stuff into my work area. It'll be out of harm's way while I spruce up the showroom."

Danny's head swiveled. "You have more space somewhere?"

"You bet she does!" The enthusiastic female voice surprised them from behind.

When they spun around, Amanda saw her across-the-hall neighbor, Lucy Monroe, the pottery lady. She was staring longingly at the two men. Her daughter Jenny stood right behind. She was also fixated on Trev and Danny.

Jenny spoke next. "My mom and Amanda have big studios just beyond that door. Mom and me make pots."

"That's right," Amanda said. "And they are both super talented." She made the introductions, noting how both Trev and Danny were inching away from the Monroe women. Lucy had actually latched onto their hands, with no sign of letting go.

"Well, we better get started with the unpacking. See you later, ladies." Trev broke away, so did Danny.

"Anything we can do to help?" Lucy offered hopefully.

"Well, ma'am, do you know where we can buy some paint, lumber and lighting around here?" Danny asked.

"There's a Lowe's Home Improvement down near the Northlake Mall, on Perimeter Parkway off Route 24. You know the place?"

"I'll Google the address, then I reckon the old GPS will take us there." Danny rushed for the exit.

"Hey, guys, let's unpack before you go shopping," Amanda said. "There's a garage door at the side of this building that opens directly to my workspace, we'll drive around there…"

"Oh, by the way, guys," young Jenny called to their backs. "Which one of you is Amanda's boyfriend?"

The pair hesitated not one moment, looked back over their shoulders and hollered, "We both are!"

CHAPTER TWELVE

Jack Sprat and his wife…

Ginny had been right about the male muscle, because Trev and Danny off-loaded her van in record time. They placed the large flowers and furniture at one end of the space, then carefully stacked the boxes of finished work and welding equipment at the other. Both men claimed to love her art, and each chose a favorite little piece. They also insisted that since tomorrow was Sunday, they would return with Amanda to help some more.

"Oh, no, that's too much," Amanda objected.

"We don't take *no* for an answer, girl," Danny said. "So let's go back inside and get some measurements."

Embarrassed by their kindness, Amanda was nonetheless thrilled to have Danny, an experienced building contractor, and Trev, with his eye for retail design, laboring for free. In the short time she'd been in North Carolina, she'd learned that southerners had a great capacity for generosity. Rather than argue, she decided to give them the small sculptures they'd admired as thank-you gifts.

"Come this way." She led them through the door leading back to her exhibit area. As soon as they reentered Space D,

Amanda saw Lucy and Jenny still lingering, waiting to pounce on the men.

"Sorry, ladies." Trev grinned as he pulled the bright blue privacy tarp along its rod, effectively blocking the booth off-from prying eyes. "From now on we're off-limits. No one gets to see Amanda's display until it's done."

"Then I'll have a Grand Opening," Amanda quickly reassured her disappointed neighbors, who looked like kittens deprived of their catnip. Once alone, she turned to Trev. "What was that about?"

"C'mon, Mandy, we couldn't get a lick of work done with those two around," Danny said. "That Lucy wanted Trev for supper, and me for dessert."

The boys playfully punched one another.

"Don't flatter yourselves." She scowled and crossed her arms. Definitely high school.

Feeling as marginalized as an orchestra conductor without a baton, Amanda stood aside, offering the occasional suggestion as the guys measured for shelves, planned the lighting, and estimated how much paint they would need. Isolated in their little cocoon, Amanda was aware of noises in the hallway. She heard hand trucks rolling, the scraping of heavy furniture being moved, and new voices—one male, one female—shouting at one another on the other side of her pegboard wall. She guessed she was getting new neighbors in Space E, and supposed her fellow exhibitors were all preparing for the June show.

As she listened, an odd sensation came over her. It moved up from her shoulders and became a smile, unforced and unexpected, an emotion she had not felt for many weeks. Losing Rachel had pulled her underwater to a place where even breathing sometimes seemed difficult, a sub-aquatic world where sound, light, color, taste and touch were muted. But here, today, something was bubbling to the surface, a lifeline of oxygen had been extended. She couldn't wait to be alone with this new sensation. And thankfully, the guys left for Lowe's five minutes later.

"We'll bring lunch," Danny said.

And then they were gone.

She waited another five minutes before venturing out. She planned to rush down the hallway, bypassing all others, to see if Sara was working today. She had noticed on her way in that the studio space Sara and Marc shared with her and the pottery women had been dark and deserted, but that didn't mean they weren't in their booth.

So she took a deep breath, ducked under the hanging tarp, and ran headlong into a large man with a barrel chest, bald head and full gray beard. The man was sweating profusely and was just as startled as Amanda.

"Sorry, miss, but you 'bout scared me to death!"

"Sorry." Amanda was flustered as they stared at one another. Absurdly, the man most reminded her of the Amish farmers she'd seen on her childhood visits to Lancaster, Pennsylvania. Must be the beard, she reasoned, or maybe the accent. He was not a southerner.

"I'm Amanda Rittenhouse," she explained. "I'll be showing in Space D."

"Jack Harris, Space B, so we're neighbors. And the little lady in Space E is my wife, June."

The husband and wife rented space directly across from one another. Amanda shared a wall with June, while the pottery ladies shared one with Jack. By the looks of the elaborate displays in both spots, the couple was well-established here. Perhaps they were longtime exhibitors currently adding the finishing touches to their setups.

"June and I have been here five years now," Jack answered her unspoken question. "We spend the winters in Pensacola then head up here in time for the Spring Spectacular in April." He gestured out to the field across the road, where Amanda saw a huge recreational vehicle. It seemed to be permanently planted, its awning poles firmly anchored in the hard earth. "I'd guess you'd call us gypsies," the big man finished.

"You live in the RV?"

"Yes, but only when we're here at Metrolina. We own a small ranch house in Florida. In between times, June and I wander from yard sales to antiques shows, picking up little treasures to add to our booths."

Jack's story reminded Amanda of the itinerate artists she had known who traveled up and down the east coast following the outdoor art show circuit, trying to make a living. It was not an easy life.

"Do you enjoy it?" she asked.

Jack pulled a handkerchief from the pocket of his green and white striped shirt. "Why not? Our kids have left the nest. We meet lots of interesting people, and the road keeps us young." He guided her toward his booth. "Here, I'll show you my wares."

His space was chock-full of antique toys, dolls, games, stamps and coins. Amanda recognized the Ken and Barbie dolls from her childhood as well as many of the cap guns and plastic soldiers her brother had played with.

"The items still in their original boxes are most valuable," Jack explained. "And that big dollhouse in the corner is a new addition. I picked it up in Charleston and I hope to sell the miniature family and furniture along with it." He lifted a tiny piano and displayed it in his pudgy palm. "Children believe I'm Santa Claus."

Amanda was thinking how she'd always preferred Robby's guns to the dolls, but Jack's comment brought her down to earth. "Well, you certainly look the part of Santa with that beard."

He gave a Kris Kringle belly laugh, then explained that as Amanda had suspected, Jack was a lapsed Amish man, not from Pennsylvania, but from a small town in Indiana. "Guess you could say I'm more like Peter Pan. I never grew up."

Next he took her across the hallway to his wife's booth. "June Harris, meet Amanda Rittenhouse."

The skinny little woman wore floral gingham, had a perfectly coifed silver pageboy cut, pearl necklace, matching earrings, and a very ladylike handshake. "Pleased to meet you, Amanda."

Her accent was pure North Carolina, and she closely resembled a porcelain figurine of Scarlett O'Hara in one of her displays. Seeing this couple together, Amanda couldn't help but think of Jack Sprat and his wife. June was peddling everything feminine with a capital "F." Her shelves were French provincial white, laden with candles, pine-scented pincushions, antique jewelry, dainty handbags, cooking aprons, quilts, and pillows embroidered with cute little sayings. In short, the kind of junk Amanda hated.

"I was born right here in Charlotte, but my dear husband led me astray." June took the big man's arm.

What a nice couple, Amanda thought, and imagined having them for neighbors would be like having nurturing grandparents in residence. "I think I'm going to like it here," she told them.

"Of course you will, dear." June dropped her voice to a whisper. "But you should pick and choose your friends carefully."

"That's true," Jack agreed. "I don't like to speak ill of my fellow exhibitors, but we've noticed some undesirable behavior from time to time."

"It's most unfortunate," June added. "But take that pottery woman. She's a divorcee, don't you know? It's shameful how she flirts with my Jack. And that pitiful little girl of hers. You'd think she'd put that child on a diet."

Amanda was aghast. Before her very eyes, this sweet older couple had become vicious vipers. Even June's fingers on Amanda's wrist suddenly seemed like witch's claws.

"The worst is His Majesty, Mr. Nose-in-the-Air Michael Thigpen, who displays down at the end." Jack spat out his venom as his cheeks turned bright red. "Mr. Thigpen deals in antique war memorabilia and considers himself an expert. Thinks he's too good to associate with the rest of us and takes offense if you call him by his first name."

"But he's not half bad compared to his simpering little bitch of a sister. Prissy Miss Perfect Maribelle and her henpecked husband Carlson Porter act like they own the place. Do you think folks have a right to act so superior, Amanda?"

Amanda backed away from June Harris. "Sorry, I've never met these people," she answered as neutrally as possible. What on earth would they think of Sara and Marc Orlando? She got an answer faster than expected.

Jack frowned. "Now that brother and sister across from old Thigpen are into recycling, or some such New Age nonsense."

"Well, they're Puerto Rican. What do you expect?" June responded dismissively.

Amanda had heard enough. After listening to the Harrises' mean-spirited gossip, she needed to disinfect herself in a hot shower. She quickly said good-bye, claiming she needed to use the ladies' room, and then escaped as fast as she could.

As she rushed down the hallway, she noted with disappointment that neither Sara nor Marc were in attendance. Their display was roped off in shadows. But when she scampered through the private office and into the unisex bathroom, she suddenly laughed out loud…

Because someone had taken the time to install an old-fashioned hook and eye lock on the inner door. No more embarrassing surprises.

CHAPTER THIRTEEN

Are you available…?

True to their word, Trev and Danny came along Sunday. All three hunkered down behind the blue tarp and got to work bright and early. Trev hung lights, Danny built shelves, and Amanda rolled off-white paint on the walls. She blocked out the chatter and dueling radios of the other exhibitors outside their bunker, determined not to engage unless absolutely necessary. Yesterday's run-in with the Harrises' had left her gun-shy. What that couple would think of her radical art, she didn't really want to know.

Unfortunately, around noon someone began pounding on the framework outside her booth and calling her name. She studiously ignored the intruder, but then he lifted the flap and barged right in.

"Hey, Amanda, everyone says you're acting antisocial. What's that about?"

She lowered her roller and was shocked to see Marc Orlando standing there with a big white paper bag in his hand.

"Hey, man, did you bring us lunch?" Danny asked.

"I brought *Amanda* lunch." He strode right up to her. "And if I'm lucky, she'll join me in my booth. She needs a break from these paint fumes."

"So we're not invited?" Trev said.

"You are not invited." Marc pried the roller from her hands. "See you later, guys."

She was too startled to argue, so she allowed Marc to escort her down the hall while the guys booed and jeered, pretending to be offended. Ignoring the curious stares of the pottery lady and the Harris couple, he fast-walked her into his booth, closing the tarp behind them.

"So…" Marc began. "What's happening?"

Amanda scanned the space, but Sara wasn't there. Suddenly she was hyper-aware of her skimpy, paint-splattered clothes and the fact that she was alone with a man who had come on strong the first time they met. "You kidnapped me."

Marc laughed and rubbed her nose with the ball of his thumb. "Sorry, you had a blob of paint on your nostril."

Amanda backed off a safe distance and scowled.

"Sure I kidnapped you. How else was I gonna talk to you? You're hungry, right? I know I am." He cleared junk from the lid of what appeared to be one of several large wooden boxes and spread out a feast of burgers and fries. "I spent the morning hauling in these window seats, so I could eat a horse. No, make that a cow. I really like horses."

She took another look at the boxes. They were truly beautiful. Some were plain with simple trim, while the one they were eating on was large as a coffin, with amazingly ornate carvings on its side panels. "Window seats?"

"Yeah, I rescued them from two different houses. Those are from a Quaker farmhouse up in Pennsylvania. This fancy one came from one of those old stucco mansions in Savannah. It wasn't part of the original architecture. I think it was carved in India."

"Wow, you've been traveling a lot," she said.

"So have you. That big white van of yours has Florida tags."

"I've been living in Florida."

"But you're here to stay, I hope." Marc handed her a large diet cola. "Why did you move?"

"Long story."

"I've got time."

Amanda gave him a withering look she hoped would end that conversation. "Where's Sara?"

He took a bite of his sandwich. Amanda did the same. She hadn't realized how hungry she was. The juicy burger, with mustard, ketchup and pickles almost made her moan with pleasure.

"My sister is working as usual. She'll be around to help out the weekend of the show."

"Sara's a psychiatrist, right? Does she have a private practice?"

Marc laughed. "Private practice? No way! She'd make a helluva lot more money if she'd chosen that route. But Sara's a do-gooder. She works for the City of Charlotte at a clinic that also offers medical rehab. Most of her clients are junkies, parolees, or abused kids."

Amanda realized she was hanging on every word. "Well, that sounds like a noble profession."

This time Marc laughed so hard he almost choked on his food. "Let's talk about you, Amanda. Word is those guys helping you are *both* your boyfriend. That sounds a little greedy—or needy."

They were seated on wooden packing crates. Marc inched closer so his knee brushed against hers. His amazing dark eyes roved up and down Amanda's body.

She pointedly scooted away. "Look, those guys are my friends, nothing more." She didn't want him to think she was a sex fiend or something.

"So you're available?" Marc winked.

Amanda sighed and pushed her food away. "No, I am not available, so will you please stop?"

He shrugged. "How'd you like that new lock on the bathroom door?"

"Good idea."

"You're welcome." Pushing back from their makeshift table, Marc wiped his mouth and fingers with one of the paper napkins. "The buzz is you've met all the other exhibitors but Michael Thigpen, who shows across from me. If you're done eating, why don't you pop over and introduce yourself? He's here today, which is unusual mid-month."

"Won't you come along and introduce me?"

"Thanks, but no thanks." Marc sounded like conversing with Thigpen was about as welcome as needles under fingernails.

Was Marc done with her, then? Just because she'd said she wasn't available? It seemed he couldn't get rid of her fast enough. "Thanks for lunch. I owe you one."

"Okay," he called at her retreating back. "I'll collect one someday."

CHAPTER FOURTEEN

The force of evil...

After all she'd heard, Amanda was apprehensive as she approached Thigpen's booth. Clearly someone was there, since the blue tarp was pulled back and fastidiously tied with a formal braided curtain rope. Theatrical lighting from clip-on spotlights featured a faux mantel flanked by two Queen Anne chairs. Crossed swords hung above the fireplace, while what looked like a Revolutionary musket was propped against the dark mahogany hearth.

"Mr. Thigpen?" she whispered tentatively.

She hadn't seen him sitting there, so she almost jumped out of her skin when a tall, painfully thin man in his mid-sixties bolted upright from the chair and stared at her.

"Who are you?" he demanded.

She quickly explained to the man who wore a tweed turtleneck sweater, corduroy jacket with elbow patches, and brown wool trousers. If he'd also worn a hound's tooth deerstalker hat and smoked a pipe, he would have been the spitting image of a southern Sherlock Holmes.

"So you're the new girl in Space D?"

Amanda did not deny it.

"Well, then, you might as well come in and have a look around."

She knew next to nothing about war memorabilia, but even she could see that some of the items dated back to the days when Native Americans used bows and arrows to stave off the invaders. From the American Revolution through the current contentions in the Persian Gulf, all the accoutrements of conflict were related to troops from the United States, so at least Thigpen was a patriotic war lover.

"It's one of the most comprehensive collections in the country," Thigpen bragged. "Best of all, everything's for sale."

She saw every type of handgun, rifle, knife, bayonet and grenade. Also badges, medals, and uniform shoulder stripes from the various wars. A neat rack of period uniforms hung against the back wall. Amanda was dying to try on a white captain's hat with gold braid, which was hooked on a peg just out of reach.

"Very impressive," she told Thigpen, who was tenderly fondling a canteen wrapped in olive drab.

"Can't you just imagine a World War I soldier drinking from this at the Battle of Verdun, Miss Rittenhouse?"

"Please, call me Amanda."

He waggled a finger at her and shook his head. "You may call me *Mister* Thigpen. It is good to observe the formalities, don't you think?"

Amanda mumbled in the affirmative while thinking that June Harris had been right. Thigpen was a snob. Even his speech patterns were a little off—a southern aristocrat trying to sound like an English gentleman. Plus, all the lethal weapons in the room gave her the creeps. While the toy guns in Jack Harris's booth had been fun, these were gruesomely real. She wondered if any had actually been used to kill a man.

"Usually my sister and her husband work with me during the shows. Maribelle and Carlson don't know much about the merchandise, but they're good at writing up sales. We made a great deal of money during the Spring Spectacular last month."

Good for you, Amanda thought, but she said, "Sorry I missed it."

"Yes, indeed, it was quite profitable, but lucky for you...for all of you...the upcoming June show will be even better. We will have thousands of buyers descending upon Building 16."

This bit of bravado did not jibe with what Amanda had been told—that as far as business was concerned, the three summer months were dead.

"You look skeptical, Miss Rittenhouse." Thigpen came close, an odd glitter in his rheumy blue eyes. He smelled like mothballs and gun oil. "You will all be thanking me, because I will be drawing those crowds. I have a very special feature planned for the June show. It will make news nationwide."

Was he planning to unveil the next atom bomb? "Can you tell me about it?"

"Oh, no, my dear. It is a secret." He touched the back of her wrist with two fingers, cold as icicles. "But if you read *The Charlotte Observer* the Sunday before we open, all will be revealed."

Amanda had begun to think the man was slightly unhinged, and it frightened her. She backed out of the booth as the light reflecting off the many sinister blades seemed to slash at her eyes. She felt claustrophobic, threatened, as though the force of evil emanated from the display of deadly weapons.

Michael Thigpen called after her as she fled. "Don't forget to read the paper!"

CHAPTER FIFTEEN

Showtime…

Thursday, June 4th, came much too soon, but Amanda believed she was ready. She had worked each day, sometimes into the night, to finish her showroom and was more than pleased with the result.

As she drove up in heavy traffic, then flashed her ID at the gate to Metrolina, she anticipated the moment of unveiling. For the first time, folks would see the sparkling white shelves filled with all her small sculptures. At the last minute she had decided to place mirrors behind the shelves so the backside of each piece would show. Mobiles hung at different levels, spinning and catching the spotlights Trev had installed, while her large auto parts furniture and funky flowers were placed center stage.

The overall effect was dazzling, with all the shiny, spinning steel and chrome reflecting off one another. Compared to the other booths, which were crowded and cozy, Amanda's space was sparse and modern. She hoped it wouldn't shock the sensibilities of the regular visitors.

She knew Thursday was reserved for interior designers and retail tradespeople only, and she'd been told not to expect many visitors. This in mind, Amanda was shocked to see the parking lot, even the fields outside her building, jam-packed with cars. A uniformed police officer was directing traffic, and even more startling, two armed cops were guarding the entrance to Building 16.

Amanda rushed past the wooden flower boxes, now generously planted with colorful impatiens—thanks to June Harris—and entered the hall. Young Jenny Monroe was directing the crush of people in to see their pottery display. The teenager looked more nervous than usual, definitely out of her element.

"What the hell's going on?" Amanda whispered to the girl.

"Don't you read the papers? It was front page news in *The Charlotte Observer*. How could you miss it?"

Amanda drew a blank. "What news?"

Jenny's eyes were enormous behind her glasses. Her braces glittered when she talked. "Jeez, Amanda, don't you know about Mr. Thigpen's Lincoln-Davis letter?"

When Amanda just stood there like a clueless fool, Jenny continued. "It was published by a paper called *The Liberator*, in Boston, on September 26, 1862. But Mr. Thigpen has the original."

"Abe Lincoln to Jefferson Davis?"

"Yeah, it's all about the legality of freeing the slaves, whether or not it was Constitutional. I read the whole thing in the paper. It's really awesome! They say it's worth hundreds of thousands of dollars!"

"And Mr. Thigpen has the original?" This was beyond belief, so Amanda did not believe it. "It's probably a fake."

"Not according to the Smithsonian. Mr. Thigpen has a letter of authenticity. The Lincoln letter and the authenticity are both framed and on display in his booth."

Well, that would explain the heavy security. "Where would he find a letter like that?"

Jenny dropped her voice. "No one knows the truth, but the rumor is he bid a couple hundred dollars for a blind box marked 'Confederate Memorabilia,' and the letter was inside."

"That guy is lucky," Amanda said.

"That guy's a bastard!" a man behind her growled. He had sneaked up on both of them. He was of medium height, muscular like a runner, with thinning brown hair, big hands and a pointed, wolf-like face.

Jenny backed away. "Daddy, what are you doing here?"

Amanda tried to read Jenny's expression, which was an odd mixture of pleasure and fear. Although it was only nine in the morning, she smelled alcohol on his breath, and the situation stirred a deep, long-suppressed memory. She thought about her brother's words: *Don't you remember how much he was drinking?* Robby had been talking about their father, and Amanda remembered feeling like Jenny, both joy and apprehension when her father had been in one of his moods.

"Where's your mama, Jenny-bean?" he said.

"She's really busy inside. We have lots of customers, Daddy. Please don't bother her now."

"Then I reckon she can use my help." He pushed past them and entered the pottery booth.

Amanda recalled that Lucy Monroe had been divorced from a man named Jimmy, and she had described him as abusive. "Will your mother be all right? Should we call someone?" She was thinking that the cop stationed just outside the door could prove useful if the scene turned violent.

"No! Leave him alone, Amanda. It'll only make it worse." Jenny was at the edge of panic. "Daddy won't stay long. I'm sure he came to see the Lincoln-Davis letter and to say something ugly to Mr. Thigpen. He hates that man."

"Everyone hates that man." Jack Harris strolled over to put his two cents in. "Ask me, Thigpen stole that damned letter. A just God would never reward that pompous ass with such good fortune." He handed something to Amanda.

It was a letter-sized sheet of fake parchment rolled and tied with a red, white and blue ribbon.

"Thigpen's selling them for five bucks apiece. It's a cheap Xerox copy of the Lincoln-Davis letter. He's also selling the Sunday *Observer* for ten bucks. He invested in a whole stack of them. What's worse, folks are buying them."

"It's a rip-off!" the oh-so-proper June Harris hollered from her booth across the way. "They should arrest that man."

Clearly everyone was green with envy. They were jealous as hell of Michael Thigpen, even though he'd brought a multitude of customers to their displays. Speaking of which, Amanda had been completely distracted from her own grand opening, and she was wasting precious time.

Quickly excusing herself, she pushed through the stream of pedestrians and ceremoniously drew back the tarp concealing her glorious wares. She hit the lights and her sparkling presentation was revealed to all. There should have been a drumroll, a stampede of her fellow exhibitors to her space. But they had retreated to their own stores to ring up sales. Yet she was pleased and proud, and perhaps it was her imagination, but Amanda thought she heard a collective gasp of approval from the onlookers in the hall.

Sure enough, moments later she was surrounded by bodies and buyers. Everyone seemed somewhat shell-shocked by her avant-garde space, but they all claimed to love her sculpture. These were wholesale buyers who expected a hefty discount, so they could mark up the items and make a profit. Amanda had anticipated this and priced her work accordingly. During the weekend, when the public descended, she would have the margin to "haggle" with people and still get the price she needed to make the effort worthwhile.

She sold two mobiles and three small flowers during the morning, but Amanda realized she was only a brief stop in the tidal rush toward the south end of the building, because everyone had come to see Thigpen's booth. Folks did take her business cards and artist biography, and promised they'd be back.

About one o'clock, a flushed and harried Marc Orlando ducked into her booth and handed her a white paper bag.

"Tuna sandwich and iced tea," he said. "Now you owe me *two*."

"Thanks, Marc, I really needed this!"

He rotated his head, took it all in, then let out a long whistle. "Your space is amazing, Amanda, and I love your work. It's even more impressive in these spotlights."

"You've seen it before?"

He grinned. "I peeked. And, of course, I saw your big sculpture when it was stored in our mutual workspace. Maybe after I've bought you a few more lunches, you'll let me barter for a small piece."

"I think that could be arranged." She needed a favor and was shy to ask, but did it anyway. "Do you mind watching my display for a few minutes? I really need to use the bathroom."

He nodded and laughed. "Sure, but make it quick. I'm doing a lot of business, the place is a zoo. Since I'm right across from Mr. Thigpen, folks waiting in line to see the letter are forced into my booth."

"That's a nice fringe benefit."

"Right. Would you believe an armed cop is stationed right behind the easel holding the letter? But don't even think about trying to see the display, or you'll never get back here."

"Okay, I'll hurry." She shoved into the crowd as Marc wished her good luck.

Good luck, indeed, she thought as she got swept up in the melee. She'd be lucky to survive this wild weekend. Still, it was really exciting.

Maybe too exciting.

CHAPTER SIXTEEN

Too much drama…

Friday at Metrolina was pretty much a repeat of Thursday. Amanda was both exhausted and exhilarated by the spectacle. As the day wore on and the public got off work, they began mixing with the designer crowd and were almost frantic to see the famous Lincoln-Davis letter. Midafternoon, two well-dressed men claiming to be buyers for Wells Fargo visited her booth and began handling her twelve-inch abstracts.

"This is interesting," the tall guy said. "Do you ever do large-scale commissions?"

The older fellow with a mustache handed her a business card. "We're looking for something like this for a new branch office in Ballantyne."

Amanda glanced at the card, her heart pounding. These guys actually seemed legit. "How big?"

"Twelve, maybe fifteen feet."

For real? She had done large works before, and if they wanted something like the piece they were holding, with simple curves and straight seams, she could do it.

"I can take the commission if the price is right." She passed them her business card, a bio and a photo album showing the large works she'd done in Sarasota.

The men smiled at one another. "Our artists rarely complain about the price Wells Fargo offers," the tall one said. "We'll buy this little piece from you today, show it to the boss lady, and then we'll be in touch."

Without further ado, the men paid for the sculpture, shook her hand, and then they were gone. Leaving Amanda euphoric. It took a full five minutes to get her breathing under control. She kept telling herself that talk was cheap, and yet…

She had to tell someone! Throwing caution to the wind, she abandoned her booth and shoved through the crowds to the Orlandos' space.

Busting in, she tripped over the large window seat and fell smack into Sara's arms. Today Sara looked completely different in a cream-colored pantsuit, rose silk blouse and high heels. Her long black hair was twisted into compliance and piled neatly on her head, while her full lips were parted in amusement and her green eyes twinkled with mischief.

"Drop in anytime," Sara said as Amanda untangled herself.

Mortally embarrassed, Amanda climbed to her feet. "Why aren't you at work?" It was a stupid thing to say, but then, Amanda seemed to get stupid in Sara's presence.

"I left early to help Marc with his design issues," Sara said. "See this? I borrowed one of June Harris's pretty quilts to put in this window seat. It adds color and excitement to the display, don't you think?"

"So *you* moved the window seat? No wonder I tripped." Amanda was on a roll.

"I didn't mean to trip you. Are you all right?"

Of course she was all right. Amanda prayed she could stop behaving like an idiot.

"I don't have any *design issues*." Marc appeared, an uncharacteristic frown on his face. "My sister left work early to avoid some asshole who's been stalking her."

"Not true," Sara said, but her eyes said otherwise.

Marc continued, "This jerk's had the hots for Sara ever since she took on one of his parolees as a patient. He comes around almost every day pretending to check up on the ex-con, but all he really wants is to get into Sara's pants."

"Shut up, Marc!" Sara punched her brother's arm. "Just because we're twins, he thinks it's his mission to protect me."

"You two are twins?" What Amanda really wanted to say was: *I want to protect you too.*

"You said Ben was drunk today." Marc glared accusingly at his sister, then looked at Amanda. "He's supposed to be a parole officer, but he's the one who should be locked up. If that pervert ever shows his face to me, I'll kill the son of a bitch!"

With that, Marc stomped to the back wall, went through to the dark work area, and loudly slammed the door.

"Sorry, he gets too emotional." Sara smiled apologetically. "How are you, Amanda?"

Too much drama. "I'm okay," she answered uncertainly.

"I hear your sculpture is awesome. I can't wait to see it."

"Maybe tomorrow? I really should be getting back…"

Amanda made a quick exit into the packed hallway. She didn't trust herself to speak one more word, because anything she uttered would likely sound moronic. Not until she was safely back in her booth did Amanda realize she had forgotten to grab lunch from the café, forgotten to pee, even forgotten what she'd intended to tell them in the first place.

CHAPTER SEVENTEEN

The lesbian dilemma…

If Amanda thought Friday was hectic, Saturday at Metrolina was chaos on steroids. The entire fairground, not just Building 16, was crowded with buyers. By early afternoon she had sold most of her small pieces, so customers were disappointed by her lack of selection. Even as she calculated how much more inventory she would need to produce by the next show, she worried whether she could keep up if she also accepted a large commission for Wells Fargo. Basically, she was running on adrenaline, so she was thrilled when Diana and Trout showed up.

She first saw Trout's head above the crowds, and then her mother's wide smile as she spotted Amanda.

"Come in, welcome!" She pulled them into her booth, deeply touched that they had come. She hadn't expected it, even though they'd both expressed interest in her work.

"Wow!" Diana's eyes widened and she spread her arms as she took it all in. "Your art is magnificent, Mandy. I really love it!" She picked up a small abstract sailboat, the only one of six left.

Trout went straight to the *Wing Chair* with the chrome bumper armrests. He sat in its crushed velvet cushions. "I feel right at home here, Mandy Bear. If I'm not mistaken, this was once a 1954 Cadillac. Am I right?"

Lately he'd taken to calling her Mandy Bear, and she kind of liked it. "I'm not sure, Trout. When I scavenged it, there were only pieces."

"Did you ever consider rigging one of these chairs with headlights or taillights? You could hide the electric switch under the arm and dazzle folks."

Amanda laughed. "You like that sailboat, Mom? It's yours."

Suddenly her mother seemed stunned and her eyebrows shot up in surprise. While Amanda tried to understand what she'd said to cause such a strange reaction, the odd moment passed.

Diana hugged the gift and gave her daughter a kiss on the cheek. "It looks like you've about sold out. Congratulations, Mandy."

"Thanks, Mom."

When her mother startled again, Amanda finally understood. She had called her *Mom* rather than *Diana*—the first time she'd made this slip since moving to North Carolina. Obviously her mother had been hurt by the vicious little vendetta she'd been waging, and for this she was deeply ashamed.

Her mother quickly recovered and said, "So, why don't you take a break? Matthew and I can watch your booth. I know you're hungry."

"We'll sell all your stuff." Trout waved her on her way. "When you come back, there'll be nothing left, and we can all go home."

Amanda didn't need a second invitation. Before this show was over, she was determined to see the famous Lincoln-Davis letter, and even more determined to spend some quality time with Sara without making a fool of herself.

As she made her way toward the café, she saw Jack Harris rolling his big dollhouse out of the building, a happy customer in tow. She saw a dozen ladies in June's booth picking through the purses and porcelain, all chirping like happy parakeets.

When she finally made it to the Orlandos' space, she saw Sara showing off the large carved window seat. Her display really was nice, with June's quilt for color. Amanda made a mental note not to trip over it this time.

"Hey, Sara, can I buy you a late lunch?" she called.

"That's not fair!" Marc piped up. He was sitting at a makeshift desk, counting cash. "You owe me, not Sara."

"Oh, yeah? Well, it looks like she's working harder, so she gets the break. We'll bring you something, Marc."

Before he could give her more grief, Amanda took Sara's arm and maneuvered her into the hall. She started guiding her toward the café.

But Sara stopped dead. "Wait, don't you want to see Thigpen's letter? I've been here two days and haven't gotten a look at it. Aren't you curious?"

"Sure I am, but we'll have to wait in line."

"That's okay, I've got time." Sara smiled.

The entrance was cordoned off with theater ropes to control the flow of traffic. The press of humanity caused Sara and Amanda to bump hips, but Amanda didn't mind. Too soon they were inside amid all the lethal instruments of war.

"Look at this awful thing." Sara picked up something that looked like a hammer. "This is a fighting tomahawk, check it out. This side has a blade sharp as a razor, the other has a point perfect for punching holes in someone's head."

"That's disgusting." Amanda had a tomboy's appreciation of weaponry, but as Sara gripped the handle and hefted the thing, even she was somewhat repelled. The tomahawk had been displayed on an innocent-looking red silk scarf. "You better put it back, Sara."

"Yes, young lady, you must put it back!" The angry voice came from a small, pink-faced man in old-fashioned round, rimless spectacles. He snatched the tomahawk with his white-gloved hands. "This is an SOG tactical tomahawk, made famous in the Vietnam War. It is not a toy."

"So sorry." Sara held up both hands in surrender. "I work at the booth across the hall, by the way. I'm Sara Orlando, pleased to meet you."

The man was not impressed. "I am Carlson Porter, Mr. Thigpen's brother-in-law, and I suggest you keep your hands to yourself."

"She said she was sorry, now can we move on?" Amanda had known her fair share of shrimp-sized men with a whale-sized chip on their shoulders, and she liked them less with every encounter. It didn't help that Mr. Porter was wearing a vintage sailor suit straight out of *HMS Pinafore*.

"That must be Maribelle Porter over there," Amanda whispered to Sara. "Mr. Thigpen's sister." June Harris had supplied the catty scoop on this woman, whom she had described as "Prissy Miss Perfect," who thought of herself as "royalty." She was tall and thin like Mr. Thigpen, with long white hair pinned up in a severe bun. She was dressed in a World War I nurse's uniform and serving a dark red punch to the paying customers.

"Is that blood she's pouring?" Sara giggled.

"Isn't it too early for Halloween?" Amanda joined in the mean girl fun, but then suddenly they were standing in front of the famous letter, which was truly impressive.

Amanda had experience as a custom framer, so she saw immediately that the precious document was properly mounted in an acid-free shadow box with museum-quality, ultraviolet-proof Plexiglas. This way it was safe from foxing, fading, and even breakage. "Nice job," she muttered. "I wonder if it's real?" She still had her doubts.

Just then Mr. Thigpen, who had been standing nearby like a proud soldier, stepped forward to scowl at her. Rather than face his wrath, Amanda dropped the subject of authenticity. She took Sara's elbow. "Let's get outta here."

In fact they had no choice in the matter, because all the curious onlookers were being herded past the artifact faster than cattle down the chute to their slaughter.

By the time they got out, both were giggling like schoolgirls. They were also in close proximity to the exhibitors' private bathroom.

"I have my key," Amanda said. "And I really need to go."

"I'm good, so you go ahead, Amanda. I'll save a place for us in the café."

As Amanda ducked into the restroom and carefully set the new hook lock into its eye, she was happy that Sara always remembered her name. She liked the way it sounded like music when Sara spoke it. She also preferred how Sara was dressed today, in a soft cotton shirt, jeans and tennis shoes. Her long black hair was loose on her shoulders and she wore no makeup. She was less the professional shrink, more like the magical Madonna spotlighted in a conical beam of sunshine the day of Amanda's epiphany.

As she considered this, she glanced again at the colorful ads framed on the bathroom wall. They were likely from the 1940s. On the left, a sexy blonde with a red kerchief was enjoying a classic Coke. On the right, a pretty brunette in pink plastic rollers was blissfully using a new, state-of-the-art Sunbeam hairdryer. Amanda chuckled:

We've come a long way, baby.

When she emerged from the restroom, she spotted Sara seated at a round table for two at the far end of the café. The joint was jumping, standing room only, so Amanda was grateful not only that Sara had snagged them a seat, but also that she'd ordered them both iced tea.

"Just what I wanted." She slid into the wire Popsicle chair beside Sara. "I like a woman who takes charge."

"So do I." They clinked glasses. "Now that we're finally alone, tell me about Amanda Rittenhouse."

Was she flirting? "Yeah, we're alone with about a hundred other people. What do you want to know?"

"What matters?" Sara tilted her head and offered an enigmatic smile.

Amanda was pretty good at reading signals, and her gaydar was excellent. But with Sara, she couldn't be sure. "Are you trying to psychoanalyze me?"

Sara laughed. It was that raucously throaty sound that reminded Amanda of the Liberty Bell. "I'm off-duty, Amanda, but it's a professional hazard. People always think I'm trying to get into their heads, so why don't you ask the questions?"

Now that stopped her cold. She had imagined this meeting many times, and while there were plenty of personal things she was dying to ask, she couldn't bring herself to voice a single one of them. "Do you like burgers, or tuna? Are you a vegan? Maybe we should order?"

Again that laugh. Sara held up a number. "Already done. I got two corned beefs on rye, with coleslaw. Did I do good?"

"Very good, but this was supposed to be my treat."

"No problem." She passed Amanda the bill. "You can reimburse me, and when they call my name, you can pick up the food."

Amanda liked Sara's aggressiveness, it was way beyond sexy—teasing, without pushing it. She fine-tuned her senses and again tried to decide: flirting, or not? Too soon the loudspeaker called Sara's name, and Amanda left the table. The debate continued while she waited for the food. Too often she'd mistaken a woman's friendliness for something more, especially when she wanted it to be so. Most likely Sara was just looking for a pal, leaving any romantic entanglement to her twin brother. It was the lesbian dilemma. Should she make a move, or would that one step take her straight off the tightrope?

She picked up their bag, the debate still raging as she moved back to the table, but when she got there, all bets were off. Because Sara was gone, nowhere in sight.

Vanished into thin air.

CHAPTER EIGHTEEN

The Karate Kid…

Amanda checked the public and private restrooms. She popped her head into Space F and called to Marc, but Sara had not returned. Left holding the bag of food, Amanda felt paranoia take over. Had Sara stood her up? Somehow that didn't feel right. She became convinced something bad had happened.

Rushing back to the café, she recognized three teenaged girls who had been sitting at a table nearby.

"Hey, do you remember the woman who was sitting with me at that table over there?"

The little redhead with braces shrugged, but the blond one said, "Sure, I saw her. She left with some dude, and she didn't look real happy."

"What dude?"

"Big bald guy with tattoos up his neck," the pretty African-American girl replied. "He was comin' on real strong, and the woman kept pushin' him away. Seemed like she was really mad."

"Where did they go?" Amanda fretted as a surge of adrenaline pumped through her veins.

"I think he was drunk," said the little redhead, who'd acted like she hadn't seen anything. "He dragged that woman outside the building." She pointed to the south exit.

Shit, shit, shit! Should she go back for Marc, or do this on her own? Unable to make a decision, she dropped the bag of food into the nearest trash can and ran out the exit. She saw six cops at that door, four more than were stationed at Amanda's end of the building. No doubt they were the security detail for the Lincoln-Davis letter.

Amanda heard the screaming before she saw anything, and soon three of the cops were running toward the sound. With Amanda on their heels, they arrived between two pickup trucks in time to see a bald thug punch Sara in the face. Then he shoved her against the bed of one of the trucks and tried to force his leg between her knees.

But Sara was having none of it. With lightning speed, she brought her knee up hard and hit him in the crotch. When he staggered back, moaning in pain, she rammed two stiff fingers into his eyes, then followed it up with a vicious fist punch to his jaw. Moments later her attacker sank to the ground, squealing like a stuck pig.

He did not get up.

Sara bent forward panting, her head down while she caught her breath.

Amanda was in shock.

Maybe someday they'd laugh about this. She'd call Sara the Karate Kid, or some such thing. But for now, she felt like weeping in relief. She reached the scene about ten paces behind the cops. One officer, a big black guy, kneeled beside the fallen thug. The other two flanked Sara, prepared to restrain her if she tried to run.

"I know this man," the black cop said. "He's a parole officer. Do you think the girl is one of his skips?"

"Nope, this is Dr. Orlando, she's a shrink at the Charlotte Community Center," the oldest cop explained. "Hey, Doc, where'd you learn those moves? You can partner with me any day."

"If these are both good guys, then what the hell just happened?" The youngest cop, obviously a rookie, let go of Sara's arm.

Amanda knew exactly what had happened. Obviously this was the amorous stalker Marc had described yesterday, the "pervert" named Ben. Marc had threatened to kill him if he ever came around, but this evening, Sara had nearly managed it herself.

"Are you okay, Sara?" she stupidly asked.

Sara nodded, but did not lift her head. Amanda had seldom felt so useless. She willed her heart to stop racing and wiped her palms on her jeans.

"Do you know what happened, miss?" The black officer turned to Amanda.

But Amanda shook her head. If anyone was going to explain this, it had to be Sara. By this time her attacker had uncoiled from his fetal position and was rubbing his injured eyes.

"You saw it, Officer. That bitch tried to kill me," he whined.

"But she didn't throw the first punch. Aren't you Ben Marsh, used to be a cop down at the Seventh District?" the senior police officer asked.

The man sat upright and nodded. He took a moment to compose himself and get his anger under control. "It was all a misunderstanding. Dr. Orlando has one of my boys in therapy. Let's just say we disagree on the treatment plan."

Sara coughed a derisive little laugh. Everyone knew Ben's explanation was totally lame, but up close and personal, the jerk looked halfway presentable. He wore a neat polo sweater, pressed chinos and polished shoes. Except for the snake tat crawling up the back of his neck, he was a clean-cut guy.

"What's the verdict, Doc?" the older cop asked. "Do you want to press charges?"

Of course she did! Amanda, filled with righteous indignation, waited for Sara to drop the hammer on this creep. But instead, Sara stood upright and shook her head.

"Oh, fuck it." Sara sighed. "Let it go. I think maybe Ben's learned his lesson."

Even the cops seemed surprised.

"Are you sure, Doc? You're gonna have one mean shiner come morning." The black officer nudged Ben with his shoe. "Have you been drinkin', man?"

"I've had a couple of beers, but I'm not driving," Ben said. "You heard the lady. Help me up, and we'll call it a day."

This wasn't happening. Amanda couldn't believe her ears. Sara was letting him off scot-free.

"Do you need a ride home, Mr. Marsh?" the rookie offered.

"I'll take a cab." He shot a dirty look at Sara. "Or maybe you should call me an ambulance."

Completely nonplussed, Amanda walked up and touched Sara's arm. When they connected, she saw a glaze of tears in Sara's eyes. "Why are you doing this?"

Sara jerked away. "Leave me alone, please."

Amanda looked out at the fairgrounds, where most of the cars and a procession of trucks were leaving. She watched their taillights moving slowly through the dusk and saw the pale outline of the moon composing itself. For a long moment, everyone just stared at one another.

"I guess we're done here, then." The senior cop spread his hands, then headed back to the detail stationed at the door of Building 16. "Make sure Mr. Marsh calls that cab."

The black officer pulled Ben roughly to his feet. Ben brushed off the seat of his pants and allowed himself to be escorted to a lighted phone booth.

Sara defiantly tossed back her long black hair and began walking in the opposite direction, toward the field.

"Where are you going?" Amanda was desperate. "Aren't you coming inside?"

"I told you to leave me alone." She turned around long enough to jab an emphatic index finger at Amanda. "And don't you *dare* tell my brother."

Seconds later, Amanda was standing alone with the rookie, who looked just as confused as she felt.

CHAPTER NINETEEN

Everyone is a suspect...

As she stood outside the Orlando booth, Amanda was torn. Marc was busy with a last-minute customer, oblivious to the violence which had just occurred beyond the door. If she told him what had happened to Sara, he'd likely explode with anger and go after Ben. Or maybe Marc would do something constructive to comfort Sara, and God knew Amanda wanted that to happen. Yet she'd been warned not to tell Marc, and judging from Sara's astonishing display of self-defense, the woman knew how to take care of herself.

In the end, Amanda said nothing. She flew to her own booth like a homing pigeon and blurted out the story to her mother. It was embarrassing, acting like a six-year-old, especially with a woman from whom she'd been estranged all these years, but oh, it felt so good. Her mother listened patiently, while rubbing away the tension knotted between Amanda's shoulder blades.

"Do you want me to tell Marc?" her mother offered. "I'm really curious to know the whole story behind that relationship between Sara and Ben."

"Let it go, Diana," Trout interrupted, then winked at Amanda, and put on his down-home drawl. "Your mother loves a good mystery, and she can't help sticking her nose in where it don't belong. But just like a terrier down a badger hole, sometimes she gets bit."

Amanda laughed. "Yeah, Mom, I've heard that about you."

Hours later, in spite of the camaraderie with her family that night at the lake house, their congratulations and comfort food, Amanda couldn't sleep. She recalled the glaze of tears in Sara's eyes and how useless she'd felt during that terrible confrontation.

Bone-weary, she climbed from bed just after dawn and wasn't surprised when the weather matched her mood. The fog and drizzle accompanied her all the way down Interstate 77 to Metrolina, so Amanda figured most exhibitors would close up shop earlier than usual. She'd heard this always happened on Sunday, the last day of the show, and that suited her just fine. She'd sold out most of her inventory anyway, so the only motivating factor was her burning need to see Sara, to be sure she was all right, still in one piece.

Ginny, Trev, Liz and Danny had promised to visit Amanda's booth and then take her out to dinner, but she couldn't even work up the proper enthusiasm for that special event. In short, she was in a funk. As she approached the entry gate, she sincerely hoped another cup of strong coffee would jolt her into gear, but then the guard rapped hard on her window.

She powered it down. "What's wrong?" This guy was usually friendly, but now he had a grim look on his face as he inspected her badge.

"You're in Building 16?"

"Is that a problem?"

"Yes, ma'am, your building is in lockdown. No one but exhibitors allowed in."

Was this some kind of a joke? "That's ridiculous. How am I supposed to sell anything?"

"Sorry, it's not for me to say."

Amanda was at a loss as an odd sense of dread built in her chest. "Well, then, maybe I should just turn around and go home?"

"No, miss, I'm afraid that's not happening." A second man, a uniformed cop, approached her window and took her badge from the guard. "You must go to your building and stay there until you hear otherwise."

The dread became panic. "Please, can't you tell me what's going on?"

"The officer in charge will explain when you get there, Miss Rittenhouse. Now please keep moving. You're holding up traffic."

"Can I have my badge back?"

"No, we'll hold onto it until the officer gives you a note of release, and then you can leave the grounds. Now please keep moving."

Hands trembling on the wheel, Amanda accelerated slowly along the rutted road to her building. The rain intensified, sending a stream of rushing water around her tires. As she neared, she saw her usual parking space had been cordoned off with a yellow ribbon of tape. Indeed the tape encircled the whole building. It flapped in the wind and glowed through the mist like a sinister wrapping on a dark steel gift. A dozen squad cars were randomly parked, some with headlights piercing the fog and red lights spinning like cherries topping a macabre cake.

In spite of the chill, Amanda was sweating as she parked in the field near the Harrises' RV. Every fiber in her being screamed out that this turmoil was about Sara. Something horrible had happened. Feeling nauseated, she turned off the engine and stepped out.

At the same time, she saw Jack Harris trudging toward his motor home, followed by another police officer. Jack was red in the face, huffing with anger.

"Don't you need a search warrant before you go poking around in my vehicle?"

"We can get a warrant, sir, if you wanna make a big stink. But if you cooperate now, it'll go a long way toward proving you've got nothing to hide."

Amanda blocked their path. "What's going on, Jack? Nobody will tell me anything."

The big man shook his wet beard. "Someone stole the damn Lincoln-Davis letter, can you believe that? All weekend the place is crawling with cops, and someone steals it right out from under their noses."

The officer escorting Jack had the decency to blush, while Amanda wanted to laugh with relief. This wasn't about Sara after all. While her pulse slowed to a rate approaching normal, it struck her that the situation was indeed unbelievable.

"How could that happen?" she asked the cop.

"Mr. Thigpen discovered it was missing when he opened this morning. We figure someone took it during the night."

Duh. Amanda knew for a fact the building was being guarded twenty-four seven. Clearly someone had screwed up big-time. "But you had men at both entrances."

"Right. We figure someone hid inside until everyone left. He took the letter, then sneaked out the side door."

"Out through the studio space? Wasn't someone watching the alley?"

The embarrassed officer stared at his shoes. "We obviously weren't watching well enough. One of the studio doors was unlocked when we checked."

"Bunch of morons!" Jack spat into the mud swirling around their feet. "I wish I could have seen Thigpen's face when he saw his precious letter was gone. Bet it gave him the heart attack."

"That's harsh, Jack. Can't you have a little sympathy for the man?" Amanda was fed up with the attitude.

"No, Amanda, I mean it. Thigpen actually had a heart attack. The ambulance took him away less than an hour ago."

It took her a moment to digest this bizarre piece of news. "That's really awful. I'm so sorry! Is he going to be all right?"

The cop shrugged. "Hope so. He was still ticking and moaning about the letter when they carted him off." He gave Amanda a hard look. "But you should understand, ma'am, Detective Russell thinks the theft was an inside job. Everyone in that building is a suspect, until we rule you out. So I suggest you go in for your interview while Mr. Harris and I search this RV."

"There were a thousand visitors through our building," she pointed out. "Any one of them could be guilty."

"We are well aware of that, ma'am."

He wasn't buying it. As she turned her back and walked toward the north door, Amanda couldn't blame the cops for suspecting the exhibitors. Everyone had been jealous, bitter, or at least a tiny bit envious of Thigpen's good fortune, so certainly they'd all had motive and opportunity. Thinking back to last night, Amanda recalled that she had been the first to leave, so she had no idea what had transpired after that.

She stepped over puddles between the impatiens, their pots overflowing with rainwater, and stomped her feet on a mat in the hall. A strange hush echoed through the building—no music, no laughter—only the muted voices of what she assumed were the interviews taking place behind the closed blue tarpaulin curtains.

Suddenly Lucy Monroe stuck her face out from her booth. Her round cheeks were flushed, and Amanda heard her daughter Jenny sobbing from within.

"Have you heard, Amanda?"

Amanda nodded. "Yes, it's terrible, isn't it?"

"You don't know the half of it. My ex-husband showed up last night and we had a big argument. Jimmy wouldn't leave the building. Jenny and I couldn't stand to be around him, so I gave him my key and left him here." Lucy began to whimper.

"So then what happened?"

"Jimmy shouted some hateful things about Mr. Thigpen and everyone heard him. Now the police have taken him downtown for questioning. With his criminal record and all…" Lucy broke down sobbing.

Amanda brushed a loose strand of blond hair from the woman's eyes. "Take it easy, Lucy. I'm sure it will be all right."

But Lucy roughly wiped her eyes and fixed Amanda with a vacant stare. "You're wrong. I see things, you understand?" She touched her forehead and stared at the ceiling, where the ever-present birds were sheltering in the rafters. "I predict this is only the beginning. It will not be all right, and before this is over, there will be all hell to pay."

CHAPTER TWENTY

Lucy's prediction…

For some reason, Lucy's prediction shook Amanda to the core. She quickly excused herself and escaped under the tarp to the safety of her own booth. In the gloom, her large tailpipe flowers looked like grotesquely twisted body parts. Unnerved, she turned on the lights and felt less spooked.

Sinking into the nurturing cushions of her *Wing Chair*, Amanda exhaled and wondered what the hell was going on. First the attack on Sara, and now the stolen letter. She didn't dare give any credence to Lucy's intimation that something even worse would happen.

Instead, she got her cell phone and called Ginny to cancel their plans for the evening. Even if the gang was allowed into Metrolina, which they wouldn't be, no one would be in the mood to celebrate.

Fortunately, Ginny answered, not her mother. Had Amanda been required to explain the morning's events to her mother, she never would have gotten off the phone. But Ginny turned out to be just as bad. She was incredulous, intrigued, and wanted to hear every detail about the theft. She kept Amanda on the line while she turned on the local television news and described what she saw. A string of reporters was camped out at Metrolina's main gate, angling for any scrap of information about the heist. So far, nobody had anything concrete.

"Are you a suspect?" Ginny asked hopefully.

"I guess I am."

"Cool. When will you be home?"

"Don't wait up for me."

The moment Amanda got off the phone, a police officer ducked into her space. It was the senior officer from the trio she'd met last night, the ones who broke up the fight between Sara and Ben.

"Hello, Miss Rittenhouse, I'm afraid we meet again."

The man looked beat, with dark circles under his sad brown eyes and a scruffy crop of silver whiskers sprouting on his jaw.

"Were you here all night?"

"Yeah, we all were—not that it did much good. Two months to retirement, and I fucked up. Pardon the language, ma'am, but I can't believe the thief got past us."

Neither could Amanda. She noticed the man's nametag "Ronald Jacobs" and the notepad he was carrying. "How can I help?"

"Well, I know what you were up to out in the parking lot when your friend had her little altercation, but I need to know everything you saw and did after that."

The interrogation continued for about forty minutes. While Sergeant Jacobs didn't seem to think Amanda was guilty, he also did not declare her innocent. He thoroughly searched her display, even removed the cushions from her furniture, and was particularly disturbed by their big communal studio space.

"It was your freight door left open, Miss Rittenhouse," he said accusingly. "Did you do that?"

"No, I'm certain it was locked when I left."

Jacobs lifted his eyebrows. "Really. Does anyone else have a key?"

"I don't know. Three of us share the space, so it's possible the same key opens all the locks."

He held out his hand. "If you give me your key, I'll test that theory."

Sure enough, her copy opened all doors. But what did that prove? Amanda hated to think that one of her studio mates was involved, and she refused to say anything that might incriminate them. Really, she didn't have much to contribute since she'd left so early, but Jacobs disagreed.

"I promise you know something, Miss Rittenhouse, so try to remember anything out of the ordinary, anything suspicious."

She realized that everyone in the building was enduring a similar interview and maybe one of them could help. But by the time the sergeant finished with her, Amanda had begun to think that everything was out of the ordinary and suspicious.

"Sorry, I can't think of anything else to say," she told him, and then she yawned.

He yawned too. "Look, I'll be around if something comes to mind, so please don't hesitate to come find me. Any little thing might be important."

"Are you the officer in charge, and am I free to go?"

"No, and no." He grinned. "It could be a long day, ma'am, so you might as well settle in for the duration."

She waited until his footsteps faded down the hall, and then she ventured out. She really wanted that strong cup of coffee, and she desperately needed to touch base with Sara. Unfortunately, June Harris snagged her en route. The skinny woman looked more fragile than ever and was actually wringing her hands in distress.

"Why are they bothering us, Amanda?" she wailed. "Those pigs practically took our mobile home apart looking for that stolen letter! Jack is furious. Do you think we should sue? They already have Lucy's drunken loser of a husband in custody. Or what about that Puerto Rican couple? Why not accuse them? Why do they hassle the decent folks, like us?"

She clutched Amanda's arm as her words spilled out in a hysterical cascade of self-righteous pity. Amanda pulled free in disgust. She remembered the hateful language the Harrises had used to describe Mr. Thigpen and his family, as well as Jack's obvious lust for the valuable letter. They lived onsite, so they had been here all last night. Amanda hoped the police would grill them vigorously.

Foregoing the niceties, she left June Harris still spewing invective and hurried on her way. Naturally there was a heavy police presence assembled at the Thigpen booth. At center stood little Carlson Porter and his tall, stern wife, Maribelle Thigpen Porter. He still wore his sailor suit, and she her nurse's uniform. Both wore the dour expressions of the stoic farm couple in Grant Wood's painting, *American Gothic.* They seemed in shock. Whether they mourned Michael Thigpen's suffering a heart attack, or the loss of a small fortune, Amanda couldn't tell. But her heart went out to them all the same.

She turned deliberately away to face the closed blue curtain of the Orlando booth. Even without a caffeine fix, her heart raced and her palms sweated. She imagined the ugly bruise that by now would have bloomed on Sara's beautiful face where the thug had punched her. And she worried about Marc's reaction once Sara had told him the truth.

In those seconds, all of Amanda's senses were heightened. She saw a lone dove fly to the ceiling vent to coo plaintively at the rain. She smelled the heady ozone in the humid air and heard soft voices conversing inside the booth. Summoning all her courage, Amanda pulled back the curtain and stepped inside.

Taking everything in at once, she saw Marc sitting on the ornate window seat with a corner of June's quilt peeking out from under the closed lid. A tall, erect man in his mid-forties wearing a crisp dark suit stood over Marc, a clipboard in his hand. The man's military bearing might have provided a clue, but the gun discreetly holstered under his suit coat was a dead giveaway. Amanda knew she had finally located the officer in charge.

He came forward immediately and held out his hand. "I'm Detective Russell, and you are…?"

Amanda absently shook his hand and introduced herself as she continued to scan the room. She focused on Marc.

"Where is Sara?"

Both men were taken aback by her blunt question, but Marc recovered quickly.

"She called in sick. I haven't seen her since she left with you yesterday."

"Who's Sara?" the detective asked.

Amanda's hopes plunged as the unease that plagued her matured into full-fledged panic. Apparently Marc still did not know about the fight, and surely Sara had been more seriously injured than Amanda had thought. Why else would she not show up for the last day at Metrolina?

"Sara's my sister," Marc was explaining. "Usually she works these shows with me."

"Has she been here this weekend?" Russell asked. "If so, she needs to come in for questioning. Please call her, Mr. Orlando."

Marc grumbled, glared at Amanda, and rose to his feet. He walked to the corner and took out his cell phone. Amanda barely noticed, because she was too worried about Sara. Maybe she should have driven her to the emergency room?

While Detective Russell paced and Marc waited for an answer, Amanda approached the big window seat. It annoyed her unreasonably that the quilt was being crushed by the closed lid, so she threw back the lid to rearrange Sara's pretty display.

The body inside was decisively dead. The jerk no longer looked halfway presentable. His legs inside the pressed chinos were improbably bent to fit the cramped box, and his polished shoes were twisted at odd angles. His bald head was pale as white marble, and his staring eyes were bloodshot and bruised from where Sara had gouged them with her fingers. His mouth was open in stiff surprise, and his neat polo sweater was drenched in blood, courtesy of the SOG tactical tomahawk buried in his chest.

Amanda gasped in horror as bile rose in her throat. She sensed Russell standing over her shoulder.

And then there was nothing.

CHAPTER TWENTY-ONE

A fucking nightmare...

It was much like being seasick, like the day she and Rachel went sailing on the Gulf. The dizziness rolled back and forth as the boat listed suddenly to starboard, and all the weight shifted to Amanda's side of the hull. As she swam to consciousness, flat out on the floor, all the people from Thigpen's space crossed the hall to the Orlando side. They were a sea of faces spinning high above her. All eyes were stretched wide in fear and mouths were moving, but she could make no sense of it.

"Are you okay, Amanda?" She finally recognized Marc's voice and felt his hand under her head. "I guess you fainted. Can somebody please bring her some water?"

She had no idea how long she'd been out and couldn't quite remember what had happened. But then she saw the corner of June's quilt brushing the floor, and the horror came back. "He's dead, isn't he?"

"Very much so," Marc said. "But who the hell is he?"

The tall man in the dark suit loomed over her. "He's Ben Marsh. Used to be a cop, but lately he was a parole officer."

"You are fucking kidding me!" Marc lowered her head to the floor. "So what the hell is he doing in my window seat?"

Amanda groaned and struggled up on her elbows as the reality of this explosive situation hit home. Hours ago Marc had expressed his hatred for Ben Marsh, but now he claimed not to know him. How was that possible?

She sat upright and tucked her head between her knees. More importantly, had Marc known about the fight between Ben and Sara? If so, she hoped he would keep his big mouth shut, for both his and Sara's sake.

Someone touched her arm and offered a bottle of water. "Have a sip, Miss Rittenhouse. Maybe you'll feel better." It was the rookie cop she'd seen at the fight and his partner right behind him. Suddenly it seemed like everyone else at Metrolina was also watching.

"No, thanks, I don't think I could keep it down." Had she actually thrown up? Looking around, she saw no evidence of such an embarrassing indiscretion, and that was one small blessing.

She had never seen a dead body before, let alone one that had been brutally murdered, and she wasn't eager for a second look. Managing to crawl up onto a nearby chair, Amanda studiously looked everywhere but toward the box, where all other eyes were riveted.

"Don't touch anything!" Detective Russell barked. "Stay out of this booth, and nobody leaves this building until I say so. We need to secure this crime scene." He got on his phone, no doubt calling for more backup.

But as far as Amanda could tell, most of the Charlotte police force was already there. She glanced at Marc, who was still glaring into the window seat, a look of pure loathing on his face.

"Did you get in touch with Sara?" she whispered.

"No, she didn't answer her phone, and she told me she'd be home all day."

"Does she live alone?" Amanda was certain Sara could use some support at this critical moment.

"She has a roommate, but she didn't answer either. Sara told me she was sick and I believed her. Silly me."

"She likely *is* sick, Mr. Orlando," the black cop said. "Your sister took quite a beating last night."

"Yeah, but she gave as good as she got," the rookie said proudly. "Does your sister have a black belt in karate?"

Marc's look of sheer surprise indicated either he didn't know about the fight or he was the world's best actor.

"Isn't that right, Miss Rittenhouse?" the rookie continued. "Dr. Orlando can sure kick butt."

Marc spun on her. "What do you know about this, Amanda? Who was Sara fighting with?"

Amanda wanted to disappear. She was damned if she did say anything to incriminate the Orlandos, and damned if she didn't—with Detective Russell breathing down her neck. In the end, she kept her lips clamped shut.

"Your sister took down the stiff in the box in one round," the rookie bragged.

Marc was stunned, but Russell was furious. He snagged the rookie by the arm and motioned to the black officer. "You boys wanna step aside with me?"

While Russell got the lowdown from his men, Marc knelt beside Amanda. "Jesus Christ, Sara got into it with Marsh? Why didn't you tell me?"

"Why didn't *Sara* tell you?" She didn't want to believe it, but if Marc had known, would he be capable of killing Ben Marsh?

"Now we have two crime scenes!" Russell hollered at his guys. "Now Homicide gets involved, as if we didn't have enough on our plate." He finished scolding his subordinates, then jabbed an angry finger at Marc. "What's your sister's address? If she won't answer her phone, we need to send a patrol car."

While Marc reluctantly complied, loudly insisting that Sara had nothing to do with the murder, Amanda made a mental note of Sara's address. Her stomach roiled and she tried to get her thoughts together.

Sirens wailed in the distance. Soon they were right outside the south entrance. Then another familiar face, Sergeant Jacobs, was at her side. Compared to these others, the senior cop was almost as welcome as a father figure.

"Now what?" she asked him unhappily.

"Well, Russell is Major Case, so he's handling the theft, but any second now Detective Rick Molerno will walk through that door, and he's Homicide. Then we'll have a whole new forensics team and, in due course, the coroner." He laid a friendly hand on Amanda's arm. "How are you holding up, young lady?"

She tried to square her shoulders and put on a brave face, but as a witness to the critical fight, Amanda knew she was smack in the middle of this mess. It also did not help that her studio door had been left open, apparently allowing the thief and/or murderer access and egress. And to top it all off, she had discovered the body.

"Do you think the two crimes are related?" she asked the sergeant.

He sighed and rubbed his whiskered chin. If anything, Jacobs looked even more exhausted than he had during her original interview. "They could be connected, but I doubt it. Whoever took the Lincoln-Davis letter was cool and careful, but this killing looks to be a crime of passion. Whoever put that hatchet in the victim's chest had a powerful personal grudge."

The assessment was so depressing that Amanda again buried her head in her hands. Something about Jacobs's gentle nature made her want to cry like a baby.

He patted her shoulder. "Don't worry, miss, we'll catch this guy. The dead man's coffin should be a trove of physical evidence. The fingerprint techs will bag that weapon, and with a little luck they'll nail the killer."

Suddenly Amanda's brain focused on that moment last evening when she and Sara were waiting in line to see the letter. She could almost feel Sara bumping against her hip, jostled by the crowd. She smelled ozone in the air and saw Sara pick up the SOG tactical tomahawk from the Vietnam era. Sara had gripped it, played with it, and left her fingerprints all over it—the same tomahawk that killed Ben Marsh.

Now she really had something to cry about.

CHAPTER TWENTY-TWO

Huevos Rancheros…

Amanda knew she was in for a long and depressing day. Detective Rick Molerno from Homicide arrived along with his forensic team of photographers, medical examiner, print specialists, artists, and even a video guy. Building 16 had already been cordoned off in its entirety, but now the Orlando and Thigpen booths were also strung with yellow tape, like little boxes of misery within the bigger carton.

All exhibitors were fingerprinted, questioned separately, then imprisoned in their booths while the techs ran around measuring, shooting pictures, and collecting trace with latex gloves and stuffing it into little plastic baggies. She didn't even want to think about what they were doing to the body. In spite of the swarm of activity, Amanda could tell the officers were discouraged because thanks to the hundreds of visitors, thousands of anonymous fingerprints, and dirt dragged in from all over the Charlotte area and well beyond, the crime scene had likely been compromised beyond redemption.

She and her fellow exhibitors were like the monkey trio— they heard no evil, saw no evil, knew no evil—or so they all said.

For all involved, Metrolina Expo was over—no more money to be made—and while tempers flared, Amanda cleaned the black fingerprinting ink off her hands and tried unsuccessfully to do some sketching.

The cops finally returned Amanda's badge and cut her loose at ten thirty that night. But first they warned her to be "on call" in case they needed her for additional questioning. She figured the request was akin to the "don't leave town" admonition always given to suspects in TV crime shows and in mystery novels. They didn't seem to consider her a "person of interest," but they clearly suspected she was holding back from dishing dirt on the Orlandos.

By the time she drove Moby into the driveway at the lake, after battling torrential rain on the interstate, she was ragged out and ready for bed. But instead of a dark house and the family asleep as she expected, she found three concerned faces staring at her from their seats around the dining room table.

She pushed off her sodden sandals and stowed her umbrella in the vase at the kitchen door.

"What?" she said into the anxious silence, and then everyone began talking at once. She knew the theft and murder at Metrolina had dominated the local news, but she didn't know it had been front page on the national channels. The family's bullet-like questions pelted her like friendly fire.

"Sorry, but I couldn't call because they confiscated our phones until we were excused."

Eyes widened as she detailed the events of the day. When Amanda described how she'd been the one to find the body, her mother rushed to give her a big bear hug.

"I hate it that you're involved in this, honey. Maybe that booth of yours was a bad idea."

"Right, would you listen to this?" Trout climbed to his feet and gave Ginny a meaningful look. "Usually it's Diana running toward danger. Now I think she's jealous not to be the center of all this murder and mayhem."

Ginny piped in. "Yeah, Diana, like mother, like daughter. Maybe you guys should team up and solve this thing."

"Or maybe not." Trout walked to the stove. "Who's hungry? I'm making huevos rancheros."

Fatigue set in as Amanda watched her stepfather dice yellow onions and jalapeño peppers. Was she hungry? During the endless day, the only happy captives at Metrolina had been the owners of the café, who did a brisk business. Between the cops and the nervous suspects they had sold out all their food, even the stale cookies.

"It sounds like the pottery lady's husband, Jimmy Monroe, is a likely suspect," Diana said. "I'm glad they hauled him down to the station. If he was drunk, envious and threatened Mr. Thigpen, it's probable he stole the letter."

"But why would Jimmy kill the parole officer guy?" Ginny objected. "Unless he got in the way…"

Amanda was too tired to debate the merits of Jimmy being the letter thief, but from what she'd seen of the man, his mind was too pickled with alcohol to execute such a plot.

"On the other hand, that Harris couple, the ones with the RV onsite, sound like excellent possibilities," Diana continued as she dumped a can of whole peeled tomatoes into Trout's salsa gravy. "From what you told us, Mandy, they are grouchy, unpleasant, and also had it in for Mr. Thigpen."

"I don't know…" Detective Rick Molerno, the head of Homicide, seemed like a thorough investigator. Unfortunately, he had focused like a laser on Sara and Marc as the most likely killers, and Amanda's testimony, grudging as it was, had done little to dissuade him.

"What about that brother and sister at the end of the building, the ones who recycle the old wood and bricks?" Ginny interrupted. "Trev told me you guys get along really well. I think the brother is drop-dead handsome, and the girl's not so bad either. Were they involved?"

Amanda shrugged miserably and glanced at her mom and Trout. They'd been there in her booth after Sara's fight with Ben and knew all about it, but Amanda had never confided in Ginny. Nor did she want to. It was a small mercy that her mom and Trout chose not to elaborate.

"Time to eat!" Diplomatically changing the subject, Trout finished browning the chorizo and tortillas, added the eggs, and then ladled on the gravy. He slid four heavy plates onto the table and poured large glasses of chilled water.

Suddenly hungry, Amanda glanced at Trout. "Where'd you learn to cook Mexican?"

"You kidding? Half the population patronizing my store is Hispanic. A fella picks up culinary tips here and there."

"Yeah, especially when Mom can't cook." She winked at her mother, grateful for the distraction.

"Guilty as charged," her mother agreed. "I can't cook. Why do you think I married Matthew?"

Everyone laughed. Amanda had forgotten the joy of family, how they could ease the tension in a crisis. Or maybe she'd never really known this luxury. Certainly the dysfunction in her childhood home had not been nurturing, so the atmosphere at the Troutmans' was a welcome change of pace. Even her seven years with Rachel never included the diversity of parents, uncles, aunts and cousins, because Amanda had been too chicken to come out of the closet while Rachel's family bitterly disapproved of their lifestyle.

I'm still chicken…aren't I? But when she looked at her mom and amazing new family, it seemed possible that someday soon she would find the courage to come out. Certainly Ginny had been more than understanding. At the same time, her relationship with her mom was newly precious, possibly fragile, and she was scared to death of rejection—so much so that she had warned Ginny not to tell anyone she was gay.

"Who wants dessert?" Trout smiled mischievously and lifted a carton of frosty butter pecan from the freezer.

Everyone groaned their refusal. Spicy huevos rancheros at midnight were bad enough, but ice cream pretty much guaranteed a sleepless night. So as soon as Diana and Trout had rinsed the dishes and stacked them in the dishwasher, they went to bed.

But Ginny hung back, pinning Amanda with her dark eyes. She switched off the overhead light so that the candle in the fishnet-covered cherry glass orb set in the center of the table made her silver nose stud sparkle.

"Okay, time for a truth session. Today was awful, wasn't it, Mandy?"

Amanda sighed. Just because she and Ginny had bonded during the trip to Sarasota didn't give the woman the right to pry.

"C'mon, there's something you're not telling me. Trev thinks you have a thing for the Orlando brother, but I want to hear about his sister. What's she like, Mandy?"

Amanda picked at a crumb of tortilla on the red-and-white checked oilcloth.

"I'm serious. You mentioned all the other exhibitors who might be responsible for the crimes, but you also said the thief, or even the murderer, got in or out through *your* studio door. The pottery girls and the Orlandos are the only others with keys."

"Let it go, Ginny. I want to go to bed."

But her stepsister had an uncanny ability to sniff out a lie or a half-truth, and then extract it like a rotten tooth. She kept staring until Amanda gave in and described Sara's fight with the victim and its horrific aftermath.

"So they'll find Sara's fingerprints on the murder weapon," Ginny concluded. "Shit, that'll seal the deal for the cops. Did they catch her at home?"

Amanda shook her head, traced the squares on the tablecloth, and refused to meet Ginny's eyes. Those eyes cut into her forehead like scalpels performing brain surgery.

"Now tell me the rest. Did Sara do it?"

"Absolutely not!" Amanda hotly retorted. "Sara is kind and gentle. She would never hurt anyone."

"She wasn't gentle when she beat him up, was she?" Ginny flicked Amanda's arm with a shiny black fingernail. "You like her, don't you?"

If looks could kill, Amanda hoped the daggers she hurled at Ginny would either wound her or shut her up. "What are you, a fortune-teller? Mind your own business."

"I knew it! Does she like you back?"

"I hardly know the woman. Besides, she's straight."

"How do you know? Who can tell these days?" Ginny batted her eyelashes and ran her fingers dramatically through her spiked black hair. "We should check it out, find her before the cops do. Do you know her address?"

Amanda, not known for her echoic memory, nonetheless had total recall of the moment when Marc had told Detective Russell Sara's address.

"I know where she lives, where she works too," she said before she could stop herself.

"Perfect." Ginny yawned, stretched, and climbed to her feet. "Tomorrow's supposed to be sunny, so what say you and me take a little ride to the big city?"

CHAPTER TWENTY-THREE

NoDa…

True to Ginny's prediction, Monday offered a perfect June morning. As they sped toward Charlotte, decorative Bradford pear trees, which had bloomed early in the spring, now marched like lime green snow cones under a robin's egg-blue sky. Ginny explained that these pear trees, with their thin spindly trunks, were vulnerable to damaging winds and sterile of fruit. Like the blossoming cherry trees in Washington, DC, the pears' blooming was a prized event, over too quickly.

"Don't you have anything better to do?" Amanda asked her perky companion.

Ginny wore a funky white cotton blouse printed with abstract scribbles that looked like children's crayon drawings, black tights, and purple clogs. Amanda wore jeans, her favorite *Save the Loggerheads* T-shirt and sandals. While Ginny was hopped up like the Energizer Bunny, Amanda felt like she'd done nine rounds with the bunny's evil uncle, the Mad Hatter.

"Well, I could be shopping for my wedding dress. After all, Trev and I are getting hitched next month. But you're much more fun than shopping, Mandy."

Sure I am. It seemed to Amanda that hanging with her was akin to being pulled around by a disaster magnet, but that was Ginny's choice. Besides, it was Amanda's inability to say no that had initiated this insane visit to Sara Orlando's house. It was none of their business. And when Ginny had explained that the neighborhood where Sara lived was Charlotte's version of Sarasota's Towles Court, the adventure became even less appealing.

"Why would a psychiatrist live in an arts district?" Amanda asked as Ginny steered her forest green Subaru off the exit to North Tryon Street.

"NoDa, named after North Davidson Street, attracts all kinds of hip young professionals. It used to be a mill town but when cotton went belly-up, the area went downhill. Starving artists renovated the old homes and warehouses in the nineties for savvy developers to move in. The place is bohemian chic, very trendy."

"How do you know all this?" Amanda wondered. After all, Ginny had only recently returned to North Carolina.

"A girl needs to keep up, right?" Ginny checked her GPS and began winding south into a residential neighborhood. "But I've never been here before. Maybe it will remind you of that place where your ex-girlfriend lives."

Amanda fervently hoped not. Been there, done that. And as they neared their destination on Clemson Avenue, it was clear the district was nothing like Florida. Instead of the lush foliage—palms and live oaks—many yards had a stripped-down look. Some of the older bungalows had been rehabbed with bright cheery colors, others definitely not. These blocks were up-and-coming, but not there yet.

As Ginny slowed and began watching street signs, Amanda's pulse sped up and her nerves twitched. Why on earth was she doing this? She flashed back to images of Sara—first spotlighted in the sunbeam the day they met, next hip bumping in the line to see Thigpen's letter, then finally the glaze of tears in Sara's eyes after the fight when she'd jabbed her finger in the air and emphatically warned Amanda to leave her alone. She had no reason to believe Sara would welcome her visit. In fact, the exact opposite was undoubtedly true. In essence, her infatuation with a total stranger was making her stupid.

"I've changed my mind," she told Ginny. "I don't want to do this."

"Too late now, girlfriend." Ginny pulled to the curb and cut the engine. "We're here now. If you won't go, I'll go in without you."

Shit, double shit. Amanda took a deep breath and peeked at the brand new faux-Victorian structure. She could almost smell the fresh lumber and the sprouting carpet of sodded grass showering under the sprinkler system. The large home was undeniably attractive, with two A-framed peaks, upstairs dormer window, cedar shake walls and stone pillars. The exterior walls were painted in tones of turquoise with touches of cream and burgundy trim. Her mother the realtor could confirm the house was expensive, but then, Amanda assumed shrinks made big bucks in spite of Sara's protests to the contrary.

She exhaled and felt less nervous as curiosity took over. For instance, who was Sara living with? She knew from Marc's comment that the roommate was female, but what was their relationship?

"Are we ready now?" Ginny nudged her and opened her car door.

Amanda grunted and opened hers. She was as ready as she'd ever be. Ginny took the lead as they wound up the freshly-poured cement walkway. Little droplets of water from the sprinkler system dotted Amanda's bare arms, raising fresh goose bumps on her fevered skin. She couldn't tell if anybody was home, because the door to the two-car garage was closed. When Ginny punched the doorbell and Westminster chimes echoed from within, Amanda's nerves began twitching all over again.

After what seemed an eternity, the door cracked open the width of a security chain. The face that peered out must have belonged to a very tall woman, for it blended with the interior darkness high above both their heads.

"What do you want?" The deep melodic voice carried the trace of an accent and more than a trace of annoyance at their intrusion.

In that instant, Amanda saw that the woman was African-American, with high cheekbones, amazingly smooth *café au lait* skin and penetrating amber eyes.

"You do not look like cops, so you must be reporters," the woman snapped. "You are not welcome here."

"But we—" Ginny began, but before she could finish the sentence, the door slammed in their faces and the deadbolt lock shot home.

CHAPTER TWENTY-FOUR

Lena Akim...

They blinked at one another and at the slammed door.

"Well, that was rude. I'll ring again," Ginny said.

Before Amanda could stop her, the Westminster chimes echoed and the door flew open, this time with considerable force.

"What can I do to make you go away?" The beautiful black woman released the guard chain, but blocked their entry with arms crossed.

Amanda decided to beg. "Wait, I'm a friend of Sara's. We work together at Metrolina, and I'm really worried about her."

After a moment of intense scrutiny, the roommate stepped aside. "Okay, I am really worried about her too. Please come in."

At second glance, the woman was even more enchanting than Amanda first realized. Being a tall woman herself, she estimated the stranger just topped six feet, and she moved with the grace of a leopard. She wore a flowing orange and brown patterned dashiki which enhanced her honeyed, mixed-race skin tones, and her shiny dark curls were banded into an unruly ponytail. Her erect stature and slim build reminded Amanda of pictures she had seen of Maasai warriors, yet the strength this woman projected was purely female. In short, she was more suited to a high fashion runway than a suburban living room.

Her long feet were bare as she glided across the dark hardwood floors, so Amanda removed her sandals and Ginny stepped out of her clogs. It seemed the right thing to do. They trailed her through the airy open interior to a black granite bar with a kitchen beyond. The visitors stopped at the bar while their hostess continued to the stove, where a red enamel teapot whistled.

"So who are you?" she bluntly asked. "Yesterday afternoon I had wall-to-wall policemen, and reporters at night."

Amanda quickly introduced herself and Ginny, along with a quick recap of why she was worried about Sara. Once she started talking, she couldn't seem to stop. She even told the roommate about Sara's fight with Ben, until Ginny gave her T-shirt tail a rough tug, warning her to shut up. But Amanda couldn't help herself. Something about the woman's eyes drew her into their fast amber current, until that river turned dark and stormy when she mentioned the fight.

"So, is Sara here?" Amanda finished.

"Do you see her anywhere?" the roommate snidely asked.

Unless Sara was hiding under a bed or in a closet, she was not in the house. Amanda gave the roommate a dirty look.

"I am Lena Akim, by the way, Sara's housemate. Would you care for some tea?"

"Yes, please." Ginny jabbed Amanda in the ribs with her elbow. "We would both like tea, right, Mandy?"

Amanda nodded as she marveled at Lena Akim's cool. If a housemate of Amanda's had been punched in the eye and was a murder suspect, she'd be bouncing off the walls. "I'm sorry about the cops and the reporters, but have you seen Sara at all since the incident?"

Lena held up her hand, indicating that all conversation must stop until she'd completed the tea ceremony, which she accomplished calmly and elegantly. She placed steaming porcelain cups for each of them, along with a dainty etched silver sugar and creamer set. As a sweet, foreign-smelling fragrance wafted through the room, no one spoke until everyone had taken a sip.

Ginny, suddenly the soul of propriety, went first. "So, where are you from, Lena?"

"I was born in Casablanca, Morocco. My mother was French, my father was Arabian. I speak both languages, as well as Italian and English, of course. And I came with my mother to the United States when I was twelve. Next question?"

Amanda was floored by the absurdity of this small talk, astonishing though it was. She couldn't decide if Lena was arrogant, or just plain dismissive.

"How in the world did you hook up with Sara?" Ginny continued. "She's Puerto Rican, right?"

"Yes, so that adds Spanish to our repertoire. And believe it or not, I met Sara at a self-defense class. As single women, we wanted to learn how to protect ourselves in this big bad world." She turned her hundred-watt eyes back to Amanda. "Please forgive the brief autobiography, but I find I can never get anything accomplished until I satisfy everyone's curiosity. Now to answer your important question, no, I have not seen Sara since early Friday morning. We had breakfast together and then we both went to work."

Amanda's mind raced. She remembered that Sara had arrived at Metrolina after finishing work Friday evening. She was wearing her shrink clothes: cream-colored pantsuit, rose silk blouse, high heels. Then the next day, Saturday, Sara had worn a soft cotton shirt, jeans and tennis shoes. It didn't add up.

"Lena, are you saying Sara never came home Friday night?"

"No, she did not." Lena turned her back and returned to the stove. "She slept elsewhere."

Now that was really interesting. Amanda and Ginny glanced at one another. Clearly Sara had another pied-à-terre, someplace where she kept an alternative wardrobe. Either that, or she'd packed an overnight bag Friday morning.

"So where has Sara been sleeping?" Ginny blurted it out, no longer the soul of propriety.

Eyes downcast, Lena poured them each more tea. "You sound exactly like Detective Molerno. The man is a bulldog. He asked me the same question seven different ways, as though my answer would change, if only he could wear me down…"

Amanda and Ginny waited for the answer, which never came.

"If I did not tell him, why would I tell you?" she said at last.

But Amanda detected a weakening of Lena's resolve. "Please tell us. We only want to help."

While Lena continued to hesitate, Amanda saw the exact moment that she changed her mind and decided to trust them. The clues were a subtle softening of her rigid posture and a sinking of her shoulders. The mist of tears in her eyes helped too.

"Honestly, I do not know where Sara has gone, and it scares me to death."

Now they were getting somewhere, and Amanda's heart went out to Lena. Friends or lovers, the roommates obviously shared history. She got the impression that up until now, Lena had been holding it all together with a very thin thread.

"Did you know the victim, Ben Marsh?" Amanda asked.

In a flash of outrage, Lena's regal bearing was back. "Yes, I met that loser at a party for the Charlotte Community Center where Sara works. The horrible man would not leave Sara alone. The more she deflected his advances, the more he pushed. She was very frightened by the situation."

"Was she?" The way Amanda remembered it, Sara had laughed it off when Marc got overprotective.

"Well, she was not precisely frightened by Ben," Lena amended. "As you have noticed, our self-defense class prepared us well. No, Sara was more terrified by her brother Marc's reaction. He absolutely hated the man."

"But Marc never met Ben," Amanda interrupted.

Lena's laugh was more like a harsh bark. "Oh, you are quite wrong. At that same Community Center party, Marc shoved Ben so violently he fell over and broke the punch bowl. It was a terrible embarrassment for Sara, who believes she can take care of herself."

Amanda was stunned because Marc when he saw the corpse had said, "Who the hell is he?" At the time, she'd thought it was improbable that they'd never met and had wondered if perhaps Marc was the world's best actor.

"Did you tell Detective Molerno that Marc hit Ben?" Amanda asked.

"Of course I did. Do you think I want the police going after Sara for a murder she most certainly did not commit? I also told the detective that Marc's affection for his sister was not natural."

The very idea chilled Amanda to the bone, and the ferocity of Lena's delivery sent Ginny scuttling away from the bar. She settled on a couch across the room and pretended to be engrossed in a pile of *Vogue* magazines. Surely Lena had not meant to imply that there was something incestuous about Sara and Marc's relationship? Amanda's mind refused to go there. Instead, it seemed more likely that Lena was green-eyed jealous of Sara's closeness to her brother.

"And you told all this to Detective Molerno?"

"Yes, I told him they should arrest him."

Whoa! Lena had suggested an extreme method to eliminate the competition. Surely such an attitude caused tension in the household, and maybe that was why Sara never came home Friday night.

"It's Monday, so maybe Sara's back at work?" Amanda said, hoping to defuse some of the tension.

"I have called her at work, again and again," Lena scoffed. "According to her secretary, Sara did not show up at work, nor did she call in sick."

Another dead end. Visiting Sara's office had been next on Amanda's agenda. All else failing, she decided to take the plunge. "Do you think Sara's staying with a boyfriend?"

This question got the biggest laugh of all. Lena said, "Are you crazy? Sara does not have a *boyfriend.*"

From her perch on the couch, Ginny waved a copy of *Vogue* in the air. "Hey, Lena, are you a model? You sure as hell look like a model."

It took everyone by surprise. Slowly, Lena shifted gears and smiled at Ginny. "Oh, I am sorry, that is another item from my standard autobiography. I try to dispense with the question upfront because everyone always asks. No, I am not a model, I am an accountant. Any more questions?"

Although Amanda had a million more things she'd like to ask, Lena Akim's response shut her down cold. Ginny too could take no more. She dropped the magazine and headed for the exit.

"Are you ready to go, Amanda?"

"You bet. Thanks for the tea, Ms. Akim."

Their hostess nodded graciously, but did not offer to walk them out. Soon after Amanda gently closed the door, they heard the deadbolt shoot home.

As they walked to the car, both shell-shocked, more little droplets of water from the sprinkler system raised goose bumps on their bare arms.

"What just happened in there?" Ginny wondered as she climbed into the driver's seat. "Do you think that bitch was all bent out of shape over a lovers' quarrel?"

Amanda sank into the passenger seat. "Who the hell knows?" She was more confused than ever.

CHAPTER TWENTY-FIVE

Keep the faith…

As the week wore on, life went back to normal in the Troutman household. Amanda's mother and Trout went to work, Ginny returned to Buffalo Guys to catch up with bookkeeping and plan menus, and Lissa went off to summer camp. Ginny's goal was to keep her seven-year-old occupied so her mother could plan her wedding, but so far Ginny was procrastinating.

Amanda couldn't understand her stepsister's apathy. Ginny was obviously in love with Trev and wanted to commit, but planning the ceremony bored her. Her lack of interest was driving her mother and Trout crazy because, as parents of the bride, they were footing the bill. Even Amanda, who had secretly dreamed of a wedding to the right person, wished Ginny would get with the program.

Amanda's traditional yearning for marriage troubled her some. Thus far her track record for successful relationships was abysmal. Still, she hoped the LGBT community would soon be successful in the quest for Marriage Equality. The U.S. Supreme Court would decide it sometime in the late spring, and in the deep recesses of her romantic little heart Amanda believed she would benefit someday, if she could keep the faith.

In the meantime, she continued to obsess over the murder at Metrolina. She powered off her laptop, on which she'd been searching the local news headlines for any scrap of information about the case, and then she stared out at the lake. She took a big gulp of her third cup of coffee and wondered how all those happy fishermen and water skiers could go about their mindless pursuits while Amanda's world was in such turmoil.

"Hey, what's happening?" Ginny was back, tearing through the house with her saddlebag purse bumping behind her.

"I thought you went to the club?"

"Forgot my phone." Ginny stopped when she saw the pile of newspapers sharing Amanda's sofa. "Don't tell me you're still trying to solve this thing? Jeez, Mandy, it's an awesome summer day, and you're turning into a zombie."

"You're right, and there's nothing useful here." Amanda swept the papers to the floor in disgust. "It's only Thursday and already the stories about the theft and the murder are buried in the back pages. All I've learned is that the investigation is ongoing. All the dumb reporters seem to care about is the stupid Lincoln-Davis letter."

"What do you mean?" Ginny was sufficiently interested to sit on the edge of a wicker chair and insert a stick of Juicy Fruit between her lips while she listened.

"It's all about the money, isn't it? The damned letter was insured for ten thousand dollars, which seems like a lot to me, but Mr. Thigpen's sister and brother-in-law claim it could have fetched hundreds of thousands at auction, and they're royally pissed."

"What does Mr. Thigpen think it's worth?"

"He's still in the hospital recovering from that heart attack, so no one's gotten a direct quote."

Ginny masticated her gum as she digested this information. Today her lipstick was an odd shade of purple, which Amanda found disconcerting. During the past two days, Ginny had speculated endlessly about the mysterious Lena Akim, and whether or not she and Sara were lovers. Her interest in the subject seemed entirely prurient. For Ginny, it was all about the sexual intrigue—was Sara gay, or was she shacking up with a secret boyfriend? Did Marc harbor unnatural lust for his own sister? And most annoyingly, did Amanda have a crush on Sara?

Amanda had found it almost impossible to silence Ginny on the subject, and as a result she found herself questioning her own motives. They both agreed Lena Akim was a beautiful pain in the butt. Ginny disliked her superior attitude, but Amanda feared her own reaction was less pure. Was she jealous of Lena?

Ginny suddenly stopped chewing. "Wait, I did hear something about the case. It was on the radio while I was driving to work…"

"Are you going to tell me?"

"The cops had picked up Jimmy Monroe, the pottery lady's ex, remember? Well, he's been cleared with an alibi. It seems he left Metrolina right after his family and went to a bar, where he got into a fight. Now two guys with the bruises to prove it have come forward to get him off the hook."

"So that's one down." Amanda never thought the man was a serious suspect in the first place. Still, she was happy for Lucy Monroe's daughter, Jenny, who in spite of everything still loved her daddy. "Anything else?"

"Yeah, why don't you try one of these?" Ginny reached behind to the table where Trout kept a phone and tossed Amanda the Charlotte White Pages. "Call Lena, or Marc. Maybe they'll have a better idea what's going on."

"You're a genius, Ginny," Amanda said sarcastically. "Do you really think I'll find listed numbers?"

"It's worth a try, right?" With that she was off, having collected her forgotten phone from the hall table, leaving Amanda alone with the silly phone book.

Ridiculous waste of time. But she got busy with the A's looking for Lena Akim's number. Surprisingly, she found several Akims in Charlotte, but none lived on Clemson Avenue. Not a surprise. Even if she wasn't a famous fashion model, a gorgeous woman like Lena wasn't likely to have a listed number. The O's were even more depressing. There were fourteen Orlandos, none of them Marco or Sara.

"Whatcha doin'?" Her mother kissed her cheek, scaring Amanda out of her wits.

"Mom, why aren't you at work?"

Her mother patted the heavy briefcase she carried. "I am working, honey. You should know by now that my job follows me everywhere. So whatcha doin'?"

Amanda explained her fruitless search for news.

"Well, you could call Detective Molerno directly and request an update."

"What makes you think he'd tell me anything?"

"He probably wouldn't," her mother answered cheerfully. "Maybe you should call Sara's mother?"

Now here was a novel idea. Amanda blinked in surprise. "Sara and Marc are Puerto Rican. Their parents live in San Juan, or somewhere."

"Are you sure?" Her mother plopped into the chair recently vacated by Ginny. "One tends to assume the children move away from home, leaving the parents behind. But look at you, Mandy. *You* followed *me* to North Carolina."

She had a point, but the idea of independent souls like Sara and Marc trailing after their parents was preposterous. Or was it? Neither twin had even the trace of an accent, so maybe they had grown up in the States, perhaps in Charlotte?

"You might be right, Mom."

"Yes, well, sometimes I hit the nail on the head. So why don't you start calling those numbers?" With that, she was off to the kitchen in search of lunch.

Amanda picked up the receiver. Much as she hated taking advice from her mother, she had nothing to lose. She rehearsed a short greeting, then called the first number. When she asked if Marc or Sara was home, a small child said no, then hung up on her. So what did that mean? Had the toddler meant they didn't live there, or that they just weren't home? She adjusted the script, asking to speak first to Marc, then to Sara. She got four firm responses that she'd dialed the wrong number, two busy signals, and one angry hang-up. She left a message on one answering machine, and was about to give up when a motherly sounding woman picked up. From her distinct Spanish accent, it was apparent that English was not her first language.

"Is Marco there?"

The woman hesitated. "Is this his girlfriend? Is that you, Annie?"

Amanda nearly whooped out loud. "No, what about Sara? Is she home?" She held her breath, and when no answer was forthcoming, she knew she'd hit paydirt.

"Please let me talk to her, Mrs. Orlando. Tell Sara it's her friend, Amanda Rittenhouse."

More silence. Then she heard the woman speaking Spanish in the background before she came back on the line. "If you're Sara's friend, you should know she doesn't live here anymore."

"Yes, I know. I visited with Lena Akim yesterday, and—" But Amanda found herself talking to a dial tone.

No matter. Suddenly she felt as carefree as the boaters on the lake and fist-pumped the air. "Yes!" She copied the Orlandos' address from the phone book and imagined a reunion with Sara—tomorrow.

What did one wear to meet the parents?

CHAPTER TWENTY-SIX

Chicken stew…

The Orlando home was not what Amanda had expected. Although it was within the city limits, the area consisted of carved-up portions of former farms in a mixed-use neighborhood. Most properties included two to four acres and neat brick ranchers. The Orlando place was no exception. The house was long and spacious, set far back from the road in a grove of pecan and willow oak trees. Beyond the residence, a large steel building bore a sign that read: *Green Thumb Landscaping—Serving the Community Since 1975*. Amanda did the math and sure enough, Sara's parents had likely been in the States before the twins were born, and by the looks of it, they enjoyed a thriving business.

She had not intended to arrive right at lunchtime, but between her indecision about whether to go at all and her angst over choosing the perfect outfit, she was running late. In the end, assuming the Orlandos would be traditional folks, she chose a soft navy skirt, beige cotton blouse printed with little blue *fleur de lis*, and navy espadrilles. She'd even added some bling—silver hoop earrings and bracelets—prompting her mother to remark that she looked "cute." The assessment was embarrassing, but she guessed it bode well for the Orlando approval.

It seemed less obtrusive to park at the curb, so Amanda did, and then headed up the walkway in her Avon Lady disguise. Abundant beds of perennials and roses bordered the lush lawn, proving someone did indeed have a green thumb. As she prepared to ring the doorbell, the gentleman responsible for the flowers jogged around the corner of the house with a hose in his hands.

"Can I help you, ma'am?" The middle-aged man spoke with a thick Spanish accent. He was as movie-star handsome as his son Marc, in spite of a little extra weight at his waistline and gray at his temples.

"Hello, Mr. Orlando, I'm Amanda Rittenhouse, a friend of Sara's. I called yesterday and—"

"Sara's not here," he interrupted. "She's on her own, hasn't lived with us for years." His welcoming smile disappeared and he did not seem inclined to invite her in.

"Yes, I understand, but she's missing. Everyone's looking for her, and I'm really worried."

"What is it, Juan?" A lovely older woman appeared at the screen door. The resemblance to Sara took Amanda's breath away. She carefully appraised Amanda through Sara's green eyes. "You're the girl who called, but Sara's not here. She hasn't lived with us for years."

Well, at least they had their stories straight, so much so that they sounded rehearsed. "Like I told your husband, Sara's my friend and I want to help. You must know the police are looking for her?"

They glanced at one another. Of course they knew. Likely Detective Molerno had followed the same path as Amanda, leading him to Sara's childhood home.

Amanda tried again. "You know she can't hide forever. Maybe if we put our heads together, we can figure this out."

"Are you hungry?" Mrs. Orlando abruptly inquired. "Lunch is on the stove." She opened the door wide and nodded toward the interior. "I am Sofia, by the way, and my husband is Juan."

"Amanda Rittenhouse." They shook hands. She wasn't hungry, but Amanda figured that accepting their hospitality was her best way in. "Thank you, Sofia."

Giving his wife an angry glance, Juan turned off the spigot, put down the hose and followed. They all passed through a homey living room with comfy furniture several decades old. Amanda saw doilies draped on the chairs, Lladro figurines, a place for everything and everything in its place. She smelled delicious aromas even before they reached the kitchen.

"People think Puerto Ricans cook like Mexicans, but that is not true." Sofia stirred a pot of what looked like chicken stew. A small cast-iron frying pan simmered with rice and beans. "Mostly, we don't like hot spices."

Amanda noticed the table was already set for two. "You really don't need to feed me, Sofia."

In the meantime, Juan began speaking to his wife in rapid Spanish. Clearly he was upset by her visit. But Sofia ignored him and lowered her voice.

"I told Sara you called," she whispered. "She said we should trust you."

"You actually spoke with Sara?" Amanda was beside herself with relief.

"What are you doing? This is not right, Sofia." Juan became even more agitated as his wife ladled stew into two bowls.

"Amanda, my husband owns a large landscaping company. All his equipment and photographs of his projects are displayed in the building. You must go out and see it. You can eat your lunch there."

Amanda did a double take. Wasn't she eating with the family? They were sending her to the barn? She was speechless as Sofia put the bowls on a large tray. She spooned rice and beans onto two side plates and added hot buttered corn bread. Next, she shoved the tray into Juan's hands.

"You show her the way, Juan, then come back here with me."

Still grumbling in Spanish, Juan pushed through the back door, motioned for Amanda to follow, and then led her down a well-worn dirt path to the steel building. Juan handed her the tray while he unlocked the utility door. He switched on a bank of lights and lit up the cavernous interior.

True to Sofia's words, the space was an odd combination of shiny vans, gleaming equipment and shelves holding the various chemicals used in their work. Everything, even the painted concrete floor, was spotless, and sure enough, the walls were hung with poster-sized photos of gardens, gazebos, even a public park apparently created by the Orlandos' company.

Amanda set the heavy tray down on a nearby table. "This is all very impressive, Mr. Orlando."

"It was my idea." The melodic voice came from on high, but it wasn't the sound of angel; it was deep-throated as the Liberty Bell.

Startled, not daring to hope, Amanda scanned the ceiling and noticed a balcony hung over the back third of the building. As her eyes adjusted, she saw Sara standing near the railing, her lips parted in that mysterious Mona Lisa smile and her eyes dancing with amusement.

"My God, Sara, I found you!" Amanda drifted toward the staircase, half afraid the woman was an apparition that would suddenly disappear.

"I didn't know you would come, Amanda, but after Mom said you called, I was hoping you'd put it together. I see you brought food. That's good, because you owe me a meal. As I recall, you were bringing me a corned beef on rye, but it never happened."

"No, it didn't," Amanda agreed as her eyes filled with tears of relief.

CHAPTER TWENTY-SEVEN

Groundhog Day...

"Well, don't just stand there, bring me my lunch." Sara laughed and beckoned for Amanda to climb the stairs. Mr. Orlando started to follow, but Sara held up her hand. "Stop, Daddy. I need to speak with Amanda alone. Go back to Mom, I'll be all right."

As Juan departed Amanda carried the heavy tray upward, careful to watch the steps instead of Sara's face. Sara relieved her of her burden and carried the tray to a tiny kitchenette at the far end of the amazing room.

"You've been living up here?" As Amanda looked around, still in shock at finding Sara, she admired the compact living space: wood floors covered with colorful scatter rugs, two bright sling back chairs and a striped futon. The walls were adorned with large abstract paintings, and a door opened to a full bath. An enormous picture window overlooked the back woods and an empty field.

"Yes, this is my own special hiding place. When we were teenagers, Marc and I fought all the time. I guess we were tired of the twin routine and everyone expecting us to be joined at the hip. I rebelled, making life unbearable for my parents, until Daddy finally relented and built this room for me."

"Very cool. You were a lucky girl. If I'd had a place like this, maybe I wouldn't have run away from home."

They watched one another through a long silence. Neither wanted to break the magic of their reunion by jumping right into the tragic circumstances leading to Amanda's visit. At least, the reunion felt magical to Amanda, who couldn't tear her eyes from the black-and-blue bruise circling Sara's right eye. Six days after Ben punched her, the bruise had taken on interesting hues of yellow and green, making her lovely face look like one half of a comical raccoon.

"You ran away from home?" Sara responded at last. "You want to talk about it?" She winked.

Amanda couldn't help but laugh as they both moved toward the chairs. "Are you trying to psychoanalyze me again? You look awful, by the way."

"Oh yeah? Well, you should see the other guy," Sara joked.

Amanda's spirits plunged. "I did see him, Sara. I was the one who found Ben's body." Each word felt like a gut punch as the horrible image of the corpse assaulted her in vivid detail. The words clearly hurt Sara too. She turned deathly pale and ran trembling fingers through the silken tangle of her black hair.

"God, I am so sorry, Amanda. I remember reading that in the paper. It must have been terrifying for you. I would give anything to take it all back."

Take what back? Amanda was confused. Impulsively, she reached up and stopped the motion of the fingers in Sara's hair. She held her hand. "What do you mean, Sara?"

"I mean I wish I could take back time and rewind the clock to last Saturday evening. You know, like in the movie *Groundhog Day*? When Bill Murray gets a chance to relive one day again and again, each time making a little change in the present which alters the outcome of the future? If we hadn't gone to the café at that moment, if I hadn't met up with Ben, maybe he'd be alive today."

Amanda captured both of Sara's hands and held her breath. "Are you saying your fight with Ben caused his death?"

Sara, looking shocked, searched Amanda's eyes. "Of course not! No way! If you think that, you must believe I killed him, or else Marc killed him for revenge. Because the two of us were the only ones who might respond that way to the fight—if we were deranged killers. Is that what you think, Amanda?"

The outburst brought back the color in Sara's cheeks and her eyes caught fire. Amanda was alarmed and ashamed. "Oh, no, I didn't mean that at all. I'm sorry, Sara. I know you had nothing to do with Ben's death."

Sara pulled free of Amanda's hands and sank into one of the chairs. "I'm sorry too. What I meant was it's possible that because of the fight, Ben came back to the building looking to get even with me. Since I was long gone, he must have connected with someone else, who then killed him. Maybe he even tangled with the thief who stole the Lincoln-Davis letter?"

It was a bizarre theory that didn't quite work for Amanda. She wished it did.

"If I could rewind time, I'd never have touched that damned tomahawk," Sara continued. "It was the murder weapon, wasn't it?"

Amanda sat in the other chair and sadly shook her head. "You'll have to talk to the police sometime, Sara."

"You mean I can't just run away from home like you did?" She tried for a brave smile. "Or maybe I can elude them just long enough so this bruise will be gone and my mugshot will look less scary when they plaster it on the front pages or flash it on TV."

"I'm so sorry, Sara. It's my fault. I had to tell the cops about the fight." Amanda was in misery, but at least she'd had a chance to articulate her guilt.

"So you came to apologize?" Sara rolled her eyes. "You had no choice, and I totally understand. Besides, three cops witnessed that fight, so there was no hiding it."

"I wish I could help."

"Well, it sounds like you've been trying to help. Lena called Mom and said you'd paid her a visit."

"I was trying to find you, Sara, but Lena didn't give you away. She never told me you were here."

"That's because Lena doesn't know I'm here. I gave my parents strict instructions to tell no one. Not Marc, and especially not Lena."

Amanda couldn't hide her surprise. She'd have thought Lena would be the first to know. Her face must have been a complete question mark, because Sara said, "Yeah, I know it's weird, but Lena and I have been going through a rough patch lately. Not your problem, Amanda."

Not her business either, and suddenly Amanda felt like she'd overstepped her bounds. Why was she doing this? As she stared at her companion, who looked sexy even in worn cutoffs, a raggedy Duke T-shirt two sizes too large and fuzzy pink slippers left over from high school, Amanda knew the shameful answer. She was attracted to this woman with an intensity that made her blush, and she had no idea what she could or should do about it.

"Okay, why did you agree to see *me*?" she said at last.

Sara got to her feet and moved closer. "I don't know. Why do you think?" She held out her hand. "Maybe I wanted you to see my little room so you could design a sculpture for me?"

Amanda took her hand and allowed Sara to pull her upright. Standing side by side, she felt Sara's heat and sensed she was in dangerous territory. Nervously, she gestured at the paintings on the wall. "Did Marc do those?"

"Yes. I think he told you he paints when he gets bored with the browsers at Metrolina." Sara ran a friendly arm around Amanda's waist. "It's just a hobby with him, but do you like them?"

Sara's touch made it nearly impossible to concentrate on the art, let alone offer coherent criticism. As she tried to understand Sara's motives, her body began to respond and she quickly moved away. The paintings were colorful, exuberant, and even somewhat violent. All she managed to say was, "Well, they have a lot of energy."

Sara gave her full-throated laugh. "They are emotional, aren't they? But let's not talk about Marc."

By that time Amanda was way past emotional, so putting some distance between them, she moved briskly toward the kitchenette. "Hey, you said you were hungry. Our stew is getting cold."

Sara followed way too close. "Thing is, most of my women friends want only to talk about Marc. Having a handsome brother is a curse. Do you have a crush on him, Amanda?"

She stopped and faced Sara. "God, no, I don't have any feelings at all for your brother." Was the woman teasing her, or testing her?

"Really?" Sara said as something electric sparked between them.

In Amanda's mind, it was a now-or-never moment. "Honestly, Sara, I'm not attracted to any men. I much prefer women."

For a split second, the time Sara had wanted to turn back stopped completely, freezing them in an odd suspension of reality. As their eyes locked, Amanda trembled in disbelief at her boldness, while Sara's porcelain skin glowed like a transparent ruby. For Amanda, it was like that first epiphany—Sara in the sunbeam—but all too soon the spell was broken.

"Oh," Sara said. And then, as if an afterthought, "Good to know." She smiled and drifted away toward the banister overlooking the utility barn and seemed mesmerized by the scene outside the far window, of the home and the road beyond.

Amanda could detect neither approval nor disapproval in Sara's response. She had worried about overstepping her bounds, but now she had jumped off a cliff. "Are you okay, Sara?"

"It's all good." But she kept gazing out the damned window. "But I think I'm in trouble."

Trouble was an understatement, turmoil more like it. Getting her emotions in check, Amanda also peered out the window and saw a dark sedan slow down out on the street. It did not park at the curb, as Amanda had done. Instead it came down the Orlandos' driveway, bypassed the house, and parked right outside the steel building.

Detective Rick Molerno climbed purposefully from the driver's seat. Before he shrugged into his suit coat, Amanda saw a shoulder holster and gun against his white shirt. A uniformed officer stepped from the passenger side, and suddenly they were banging on the door.

Amanda's mouth went dry and Sara's hands gripped the banister until her knuckles turned white. "I'm sorry, Amanda," she said. "It looks like our lunch will have to wait."

CHAPTER TWENTY-EIGHT

The Saturday Morning Girls' Hike...

"So, did they arrest her?" Ginny called back over her shoulder as they climbed uphill.

"I don't know. They just came and took her away." Amanda was bringing up the rear, while her mother and Ursie were up front as they entered the last mile of what was intended to become a new tradition: The Saturday Morning Girls' Hike.

"Well, did they read Sara her Miranda rights?" her mother panted. It seemed that she would become the leader of these hikes, with more energy than the two women who were twenty-some years younger.

"I didn't hear them read her rights, but they might have done it in the car." Amanda was exhausted from her ordeal the day before and worried about Sara. "What happens next?"

"Depends on the evidence," her mother said. "If the police and district attorney feel like they have enough to go for a conviction, the DA will call a grand jury and try to get an indictment. If they get an indictment, the accused can plead guilty and get a plea bargain, or not guilty and go to trial."

"You're a legal encyclopedia, Mom. Did you learn all that from the TV crime shows?"

"Believe it or not, Amanda, your mom has been in court several times. Dad says she's a crime show waiting to happen." Ginny smiled proudly. "And if this past week is any indication, you're following in her footsteps."

The only footsteps Amanda cared to follow were the ones on this hike. As she brought up the rear, Lake Norman glistened to her right while undeveloped forest rose on the hillside to her left. The perfect summer morning was a direct contrast to the past stormy weekend at Metrolina, where she'd witnessed the fight on Saturday then learned about the stolen letter and found a dead body on Sunday. It seemed impossible that a person's life could change so drastically in one short week.

Her companions had promised that this vigorous hike would sweat out her stress and clear the cobwebs from her mind. Amanda hoped so, because her sleep-deprived body and cluttered brain required a complete overhaul.

Yesterday, before Detective Molerno and his sidekick took Sara away, they'd read the riot act to both Amanda and Sara's parents for obstruction. Amanda had wanted to defend Sara by explaining how her fingerprints got on the murder weapon, but she didn't want to volunteer that information on the off chance they hadn't been found. So in the end, she kept quiet.

Before they took her away, Sara had begged unsuccessfully to change from her grubbies to street clothes, clinging to a modicum of pride in the face of indignity. She'd seemed so small, shrunken even, when the cops marched her down the stairs. In the meantime, poor Juan was impotent to protect his daughter, and Sofia wept.

Sara had never once met Amanda's eyes as they left, and once she was gone, Juan had accused Amanda of leading the cops to their door. She'd told him that was impossible. No way had they followed her. Yet by the Orlandos' expressions, they didn't quite believe her, and that was a cruel cut indeed.

"Was she in handcuffs?" Ginny asked as they all paused at the top of a rise.

"No, they did not use handcuffs."

"So, is Sara a good friend of yours now?" Her mother was curious.

"I hope so, Mom." But in truth, Amanda was more confused than ever about their relationship. Before the cops came, she'd felt sure something momentous was about to happen between them, but then she'd been wrong before when it came to those things.

"Yeah, Mandy, how's it going between you and Sara?" Ginny teased.

Amanda shot her a warning look. The last thing she needed was more sexual innuendo from Ginny, especially in front of her mother. Luckily, a cell phone rang, disrupting the moment. Her mother and Ginny always carried their phones, but Amanda seldom did, so it took several rings before she realized the clamor was coming from her own pocket. She'd brought the phone today hoping to hear from the Orlandos, but when she answered, a vaguely familiar male voice came on the line.

"It's Peter Smith from Wells Fargo. Do you remember me?"

She didn't remember his name, but she sure as hell remembered the offer. This was the older of the two guys, the one with the mustache, who had expressed an interest in commissioning a large sculpture.

"Of course I remember you, Mr. Smith."

"Well, we showed your little sailboat to the boss lady, and she was quite impressed. We'd like to commission that twelve-foot sculpture for our new branch office. If the price is right, we'll sign a contract. When can we meet?"

Amanda was speechless. She had never landed a substantial commission on her own. She'd always relied on Rachel to make those connections for her.

"Bankers don't work on Saturdays, do they?" she asked.

Peter Smith laughed. "No, they don't, but I'm not a banker. I'm in charge of art acquisitions, so it's weekends when I'm on the prowl. Why don't we meet this morning, your booth at Metrolina?"

Amanda glanced at her phone. It was already ten o'clock. She needed a quick shower and an hour of travel time. "Would noon work for you?"

"Yes, ma'am, it's a date. See you there."

This could be just the distraction she needed, not to mention a money transfusion when her finances were on life support. Besides, she needed a good excuse to return to the scene of the crimes. With luck, she'd run into Marc Orlando and get an update.

"Guess what?" she exclaimed. Her mother was doing stretch exercises and Ginny was filing her nails. "That was the guy from Wells Fargo. I got the commission!"

"That's wonderful, honey!" Her mother gave her a big hug.

Ginny said, "Very cool. How much are they paying you?"

"I don't know yet, but I'm meeting the man at noon, at Metrolina, so I've got to hurry."

"I'm coming with you," Ginny said. She still hadn't forgiven Amanda for being excluded from yesterday's adventure.

"No, you are not going," her mother interrupted. "We are shopping for your wedding dress today, and I won't take no for an answer."

Ginny was crestfallen, but everyone knew there was no arguing with Diana Rittenhouse. Amanda was glad, because from now on she wanted to fly solo.

"Race you to the cottage!" she hollered, and took off ahead of them, fueled by a burst of new energy and purpose.

CHAPTER TWENTY-NINE

Dumpster diving…

Peter Smith was waiting for her outside Building 16. He was pacing restlessly and, by his grim expression, was not too happy.

Amanda checked her watch—she was right on time. "I'm so sorry, Mr. Smith. Have you been here long?"

"Please call me Peter, and that's not the problem." His wide gesture included the surrounding parking lot, where a gang of teenage boys in scout uniforms swarmed like brown locusts. "These kids are Law Enforcement Explorers, and that little boy with the glasses wouldn't allow me into the building."

Amanda had never heard of such a thing. "What are they doing?"

"Dumpster diving, by the looks of it."

Sure enough, the scouts were currently standing on wooden crates unloading garbage from the bin behind the Harrises' RV. The wind had picked up, sending little bits of paper and cardboard everywhere.

"They don't seem too organized," she said.

"Organized enough to throw their weight around. Did you know your building's been in lockdown all week? Apparently the police have searched the inside, and now their little deputies are finishing up the dirty work."

"I didn't know."

Just then the north door opened and Detective Russell poked his head out. "You and your guest can come in now, Miss Rittenhouse. Sorry for the inconvenience."

She quickly helped Peter Smith duck under her blue tarp curtain, turned on the lights, and took him straight to her desk.

"Terrible mess here last weekend," Peter commented.

Amanda didn't want to dwell on the negative. "Yes, but something good happened too—my opportunity to work with Wells Fargo."

"We're lucky we found you." Peter opened his briefcase and they got down to business. He presented her with a contract specifying the general size of the sailboat commission. The payments were to be made in three parts: ten thousand at signing, ten thousand with the presentation of approved sketches—due in one month, and a whopping thirty thousand upon completion at Christmas.

Amanda nearly choked on her good fortune. She had never ever earned anything like fifty thousand dollars in one, even two years! This huge windfall would support her for quite a long time.

"Wow, thank you, Peter!" Much as she wanted to play it cool, she could not. She gave him a hug, signed the contract and accepted her first check.

"Glad you approve, and I'll see you again next month for the sketches. I'm sure they'll be great."

Five minutes later, he was gone and Amanda was on her cell phone. Her mother was first to receive the news, and they both squealed with delight. Next Trout and Ginny—more shouts of congratulations.

Amanda was still in shock. She did a little dance in her booth, tucked her check into her wallet and locked it in a drawer. The euphoria did not wear off until she heard shouting and running in the hallway.

The running sounded more like a stampede. What the hell was going on? She rolled back her curtain and saw the herd of Boy Scouts rushing toward Detective Russell, almost toppling the big man. Lucy Monroe, Jack and June Harris, and even Maribelle and Carlson Porter from the Thigpen booth emerged to see what all the fuss was about. Amanda noted with disappointment that Marc Orlando was not among the onlookers.

"Calm down, boys. What have you found?" Russell, head of the Major Case Squad, attempted to control the youngsters.

The small kid with glasses, who seemed to be the leader, held a flat rectangular object high aloft in his gloved hand.

"Look, we found the Lincoln-Davis letter!" he screamed.

A collective gasp went up from the crowd, and Amanda pressed as close as she could along with the others. These scouts were much more professional than she'd imagined. All wore gloves to gather evidence, and what a find they'd made!

Detective Russell pulled on his own pair of latex gloves and took the frame from the boy by its edges. Walking aside, he carefully blew some accumulated dirt off the glass, and his face fell. Those close enough could clearly see what Amanda had suspected: If it's too good to be true, it probably isn't.

Russell shook his head in disgust. "Nice job, boys, but the frame is empty. Someone removed the letter and then threw this away."

The scouts groaned in disappointment, and Amanda strained for a closer look. Even at a distance, she could see that this was indeed the frame that had contained the letter. She recognized not only the molding but also the distinct shadowbox design and museum glass. Too bad.

"Where exactly did you find this, fellas?" Russell asked.

Several scouts pointed at Jack Harris, who seemed to be hiding behind his big Amish beard. "It was in the Dumpster right behind that man's mobile home!" the leader said.

All eyes swiveled to Jack, whose bald head turned red.

"You know anything about this, Mr. Harris?"

"No, sir!" Jack said defiantly.

"What's wrong with you people?" June Harris's voice was shrill as she pounded her skinny fists against Russell's chest.

"How can you be so stupid? Do you think my husband would be crazy enough to dump the evidence in his own backyard?"

Good point, Amanda thought. On the other hand, even brilliant criminals screw up when they get rattled.

Russell contained June's flying fists in one large paw. "What about you, ma'am? Do you know how this frame came to be in your trash?"

Without warning, June spat on Russell's tie and jerked free, prompting Amanda to wonder if this woman who pretended to be such a fine lady was merely a tramp in disguise.

"Didn't that woman just assault an officer?" one of the scouts asked.

Russell laughed. "I think we can let her off with a warning, son. Now everyone please go about your business. We will process this evidence, then take it from there."

"Excitement's over, folks," the officious little boy with the glasses said. "Remember, everyone's innocent until proven guilty."

His pronouncement brought more laughter as everyone returned dutifully to their spaces. In the chaos, Amanda had almost forgotten that she would soon be rich. She wished she could share that news with Sara. And then she began worrying all over again. Had Sara been released, or was she suffering in jail?

The idea brought her down like a plane crash as she sank into her *Wing Chair* and buried her face in her hands.

CHAPTER THIRTY

A strip of cardboard...

Eventually Amanda realized she needed to come to grips with her warring emotions. She must organize her thoughts and do something constructive. Her mother had packed her a cooler with a makeshift lunch, so Amanda decided to eat it in her studio. Afterward she'd do inventory of the welding materials on hand and determine what she needed to buy to replenish her stock of small sculpture in time for the next show.

She pulled open the door at the end of her booth and entered her workspace. Instead of turning on the strong lights, she walked across the room to open the utility door leading to the alley. She figured it would be much more relaxing to sit in a pool of natural sunshine and enjoy her lunch.

As she unlocked the deadbolt and pushed the pressure bar, she realized the door was self-locking to the outside, even when unlocked on the inside.

She dragged over a crate to prop it open, allowing the refreshing wind to blow in. As she twisted off the lid of the plastic bowl of Waldorf salad, then dug in with a spoon, it occurred to her that the door actually worked this way. Likely it was a fire regulation. Whoever was inside could easily escape once they'd unlocked the door, but they'd also be safe from outside intruders. Amanda made a mental note to never leave her key inside even if it appeared the door was unlocked, because if she was working alone, she'd never get in again.

As she finished the salad and polished off a bottle of iced tea, she again wondered how the thief/killer had used her door that fateful night. It was obvious that the criminal needed a key to get in or out, so the suspects were limited to herself, Lucy and Jenny Monroe, and Marc and Sara Orlando. It was easy to eliminate the first suspect, and the pottery women seemed unlikely, so the crime was down to Marc or Sara.

She just didn't buy it.

As she bent over to capture a paper napkin that had blown off her lap, Amanda noticed a strip of cardboard. It was about one inch wide and six inches long, lying on the floor near the crate where she sat. Curious, she picked it up and held it to the light. It was perfectly ordinary except for a small indentation about one half inch square.

Because she had been obsessing about the doors, she held the scrap up to the lock mechanism and saw that the indentation perfectly matched the latch bolt that tongued into the strike plate. Yes! Someone had used the piece of cardboard to keep the door from locking. Positioned correctly, it would not be noticeable from either inside or out.

So one or more of the crimes had definitely been premeditated. She shivered involuntarily. This meant the intruder had not necessarily been one of the tenants, but could have been any visitor to Metrolina who managed to sneak into the studio space while her door was open. Her space, her door—the intrusion felt like a personal violation.

While she absorbed this terrifying thought, she heard a door scrape open directly behind her. Someone hit the switch, and the room was ablaze with light. Amanda saw the menacing dark figure only in silhouette, and just as she opened her mouth to scream, the man spoke:

"Sorry, Miss Rittenhouse. I didn't mean to scare you."

She recognized Detective Russell and felt like a fool.

"Did I interrupt your lunch?"

She couldn't speak until her heart stopped racing.

"Why don't we both step back into your showroom? I have some questions looking for answers."

Russell's blunt suggestion did nothing to slow her pulse, but Amanda obediently closed up her cooler, slid the scrap of cardboard into her pocket, and very deliberately locked her utility door. But when she approached the man on wobbly legs, he was not moving into her showroom, but rather pacing along the inner wall.

"I see three doors here," he said. "What's the story, Miss Rittenhouse?"

Before she could answer, Russell shoved the middle door leading to June Harris's space. It flew open of its own volition, but stopped against something inside the booth.

"June Harris is in there, right?" he barked. "I understand she doesn't rent workspace like you, the Monroe women, and Marc Orlando. So how come she has access?"

"How should I know? I just rented my space." She peeked around him and saw the backside of a large display cabinet, with only a two-foot passageway between it and the door. A skinny woman like June could easily squeeze through into the workspace.

Just then June herself appeared from around the cabinet. She was so furious Amanda wondered if she'd spit at Russell again.

"What the hell do you want now?" she snapped.

"How often do you sneak into these studios, Mrs. Harris?" Russell mildly inquired.

"Never!" She slammed the door in their faces and shoved the heavy cabinet against it.

Russell chuckled. "Jesus, that's a strong little lady with a big temper."

Amanda followed the detective to the Orlando door. It too swung open without resistance.

"What's wrong with you people? Why don't you have locks on your pass-through doors?"

Amanda had no answer.

Instead of returning to her showroom, as Russell had originally suggested, he stomped into the Orlandos' dark booth, and she followed.

"I don't get it. Don't you have things of value in your studios? I will speak with management today and locks will be in place tomorrow," he finished testily.

Amanda figured that was like closing the stable door after the horse had bolted, but she didn't say so. She was sick to death of worrying about doors and disappointed all over again that Marc wasn't around. Maybe it would help if she gave Russell her precious piece of evidence. She handed him her scrap of cardboard.

"What's this?" He frowned at the clue in the palm of his hand.

She took a deep breath and explained in detail.

He shrugged disdainfully. "So what? My men never found this, and they did a thorough sweep. Hell, maybe one of my guys stuck that in your door so he could step outside for a smoke. Point is, without a timeline and a chain of evidence, it's meaningless."

Amanda wanted to kick his well-dressed shins. "No, you're wrong. It proves that anybody could have gained access to the entire building. It proves the crimes were not necessarily an inside job, and it means that someone like Sara Orlando cannot be implicated just because she works here."

"I appreciate your interest in the case, ma'am, but I'm not here to question you about doors." He pointed at the chair next to where the big window seat used to be—the window seat now conspicuously missing.

"You better sit down. This could take a long time. I want to discuss the Lincoln-Davis letter." Russell pulled up a chair for himself.

"I don't know anything about the letter."

"Don't be too sure. May I call you Amanda?" He pushed on without waiting for her permission. "I want you to think back to last Sunday morning when you arrived at Metrolina and heard that the letter was missing."

Her mind drifted back to the rain, puddles in the dirt, and yellow crime tape flapping in the wind.

"I assume you arrived at the fairgrounds on time that morning, and by then Building 16 was in lockdown," Russell continued. "But we didn't prevent the exhibitors from leaving the building with personal items until almost noon. Do you remember that, Amanda?"

It was blurred in her mind, the four days of the show running together, but she did recall the officers searching her purse when she left the building that night.

"Building 16 has been guarded day and night since the theft, no exceptions. We've thoroughly checked the interior, and now that the empty frame has been found outside, we're wondering if anyone saw someone carrying something out before noon Sunday morning."

"Honestly, Detective, don't you think the letter was stolen in the middle of the night before? It seems pretty obvious that the thief sneaked in and out through the alley freight door, so the crime was a done deal before we opened Sunday morning."

He fiddled with one of his cufflinks. "You're probably right, Amanda, but please answer the question."

She racked her brain and finally remembered that after being interviewed by Sergeant Jacobs, she'd badly needed a cup of coffee and had headed down toward the café. This had occurred before noon. Along the way she'd encountered a distressed June Harris. The woman was wringing her hands and ranting about how unfairly the cops had treated them by searching their mobile home. At that moment, Amanda had seen something else.

"Wait, I do remember something, Detective. I saw Jack Harris Sunday morning. You'd already been through his RV, and he'd come back into the building…"

"Yes?"

"He was heading back outside with a stack of those flat cardboard Express Mail envelopes in his hands."

Russell snapped to attention. "How many envelopes? UPS, FedEx or US Mail?"

She shook her head. "I don't recall." It didn't stretch the imagination to picture the stolen letter in one of those packages. "But it doesn't prove anything. I know for a fact that Jack sells and ships vintage prints to buyers all over the country." The last thing Amanda wanted was to implicate another fellow exhibitor.

But it was too late. Russell was on his feet, striding down the hallway. "You've been a great help, Amanda. I'll have a little talk with Mr. Harris right now."

CHAPTER THIRTY-ONE

A crazed banshee…

Amanda hated herself. Except for the astonishing good fortune of her Wells Fargo commission, she never should have visited Metrolina today. She should have kept hiking with her mother, Ginny and Ursie. At least then, removed from civilization, she couldn't hurt anybody. So far she'd managed to make a fool of herself over a scrap of cardboard. The Harrises were already pissed because the Lincoln-Davis frame had been discovered in their Dumpster. Amanda and Detective Russell had pushed their way through the back door of June's booth, infuriating the woman. And now Amanda had all but accused Jack of smuggling the stolen letter out in a mailing envelope.

Like Rachel always said: "Amanda, you sure know how to lose old friends and make new enemies."

So be it. After all, what if June Harris had indeed stolen the letter? She gazed across the gloomy hallway to the Thigpen booth, which was lit up like a birthday cake. Michael Thigpen's sister Maribelle and her husband Carlson were taking inventory.

Without his *HMS Pinafore* sailor suit, and she without her World War I nurse's uniform, the couple looked almost normal, and younger somehow. Amanda detected a harmony between them that had been missing when the formidable Michael Thigpen had been present.

Still, in light of the theft and Mr. Thigpen's heart attack, it seemed odd that the pair was working so diligently when their issues remained unresolved.

Not your business, Amanda firmly told herself. In spite of an urgent need to pee, she was unwilling to walk through the Thigpen booth to the private bathroom. Fortunately, the public restrooms behind the café were open to accommodate the continuing police presence, so Amanda availed herself of those facilities and felt much better.

When she returned to the Orlando booth and started to sit down, she realized she could camp out there all day but that wouldn't make Marc appear. Indeed, being there only intensified her worries about Sara, so best she get busy and do something. Yet she knew she'd be unable to concentrate on her own inventory, so maybe she'd done enough for one day—all of it counterproductive.

She decided to go home.

Keeping her head down, she walked up the center of the hallway, but could not ignore the angry shouting from Jack Harris's booth, where Jack was being grilled by Detective Russell. She was almost home free when June Harris sprang forward like a crazed banshee and latched onto Amanda's wrist.

"How could you do this to us, you little bitch? We thought you were an ally, but now you've told that policeman my husband stole the letter!"

The woman was out of control and Amanda was truly alarmed. June's face was a shade of apoplectic purple, and when she cocked her elbow and drew back her opened hand, Amanda closed her eyes and prepared to be slapped.

Instead, she heard a short scuffle, and when she opened her eyes, Jenny Monroe had grabbed June's arm and wrestled her a few paces down the hall.

"Calm down, Mrs. Harris!" the girl shouted. "I'm sure Amanda never told the policeman any such thing."

"No, I didn't. I promise. He just jumped to the wrong conclusion," Amanda blurted in self-defense. She was ashamed of allowing a teenager to fight her battle, yet she was thrilled by the support. "I'm sure your husband will be okay," she finished lamely.

"You're gonna be sorry, Amanda Rittenhouse!" June shook a fist in her face. "If I were you, I'd watch my back."

June jerked free of Jenny's grip and stomped into her booth, noisily closing her blue curtain behind her.

"What a witch!" Jenny huffed. "Long as I've known her, that old lady's had a burr up her ass."

Amanda was still shaken. "Thanks for your help, Jenny, but now I better get going—"

"No, wait! I really need to talk to you. Can you come into our booth a minute?"

Now what? Amanda longed to be gone from this place, yet she owed Jenny. When they stepped inside, the first thing she noticed was that so many pots had been sold during the show, the shelves were depleted. The second thing she noticed was that Jenny's mom was nowhere in sight.

"I'm really glad that your father was cleared of all suspicion," Amanda began as they both took seats in the corner near Jenny's display of fantasy animals.

"Yeah, me too." Jenny's broad smile showed off her sparkling braces. "Daddy's a mess, but he'd never steal that dumb letter."

"So, how can I help, Jenny?"

The girl was suddenly shy, twisting her fingers as she searched for the right words. "Well, I've heard what they've been saying about you, Amanda. Everyone thinks you left your freight door unlocked, and that's how the criminals got in."

Amanda wondered who all had been talking, but waited patiently for Jenny to continue.

"That's not right, and I feel bad because I think it's all my fault." Jenny picked up one of her pieces, a little pink unicorn.

"See, I've been sneaking out your door to smoke. I use that little piece of cardboard you found to keep the door from locking until I get back in, you know?"

Amanda did not know. She also wondered how everybody knew about her cardboard clue. "I don't get it, Jenny. How come you don't use your own freight door?"

"Are you kidding? Mom would find out. She'd find my cigarette butts, or something. I used her key to open your door."

Amanda stared at the pink clay unicorn as all her carefully deduced theories went up in smoke. She didn't know what to say to the kid.

"Hey, do you like this crazy critter, Amanda?" Jenny handed her the little figurine. "I want you to keep it. A gift. You won't tell Mom about the cigarettes, right?"

"Right. I won't tell her." Amanda tried to smile. "Don't you have your own set of keys to our workspace?"

Jenny moaned. "I, like, lost my keys about three weeks ago. Mom would kill me if she found out."

God damn! Amanda's theories flushed all the way down the toilet. Now she knew that somewhere in the big bad world, a killer was walking around with his own set of keys. He had no need of a cardboard scrap, thank you very much, because he could come and go freely.

"I don't suppose you know where you lost them?"

Jenny scratched her head. "I think I lost them here someplace, maybe even left them in the keyhole. But I can't be sure."

Amanda felt like crying. "Well, don't worry about it, Jenny. I'll make you a copy of my key when I get a chance, and your mom will never know the difference. But listen, you need to tell the police you lost the key."

Jenny nodded solemnly.

"I love my unicorn, by the way. Thanks." Amanda smiled.

"You're welcome."

One minute later, Amanda ducked into her booth, emotionally exhausted. She headed directly to her desk, to unlock her purse and get out of there. But when she bent over her desk her entire body recoiled in horror. The bird lying on its surface was deader than dead. The dove's little legs stuck straight up in the air and its beady eyes stretched wide open in surprise. Worst of all, its head had been neatly cut off its body.

Amanda screamed bloody murder.

CHAPTER THIRTY-TWO

A perfect blue sky…

Amanda lay on her back in the hull of Trout's rowboat, her head on a boat cushion in the bow, her legs hooked over the middle seat. She watched feathery cumulus clouds skitter across a perfect blue sky and listened to the rhythmic dip and splash as her mother worked the oars. They were alone in the middle of Lake Norman, with Ursie curled up in the stern, but Amanda was not at peace.

She was on the edge of tears as she worried about Sara and tried not to see agonized faces forming and disassembling in the innocent clouds. As a child she'd seen Grandpa Whitaker, beard and all, calling to her from the clouds for days after his death. When pets died—dogs, cats, rabbits, turtles—they all haunted her from the sky and she was still half convinced that was how lost souls communicated.

"You're quiet today, Mandy." Her mother gave her a little nudge with her bare foot. "Are you okay?"

Tears pressed behind her eyes. Her mother had been aware of her cloud fears. She had tried to convince her that the formations were benign manifestations, like angels watching over her—but young Amanda never bought it.

"I'm fine, Mama," she said.

"Did you just call me *Mama*? Now I know something's wrong." Her mother stopped rowing and stared at her through watery blue eyes.

Amanda was mortified. She shifted up onto her elbows and stared back as her emotions raged. "You *are* my mama," she slowly began, "and I am so sorry for the way I've behaved. From the moment I arrived in North Carolina, I've treated you badly. Can you forgive me?"

Her mother held up her hand and shook her head. "Please stop, Mandy. Believe me. I understand. We lost each other, didn't we, and I'm to blame. You were a hurt child when you ran away, but I was an adult and should have come after you. Can *you* forgive *me*?"

They both cried as waves gently rocked them. Her mother reached out and took Amanda's hands and Amanda held on. Her mother was the life raft in a sea of tumultuous resentment that had threatened to drown her for way too many years.

"I love you, Mom."

"I love you more." Her mother echoed the mantra that had been their mainstay throughout the long ago happy years.

In the meantime, Ursie became increasingly distressed that the overwrought humans would soon hug and capsize the boat. She shoved her long nose between them and batted their hands apart.

They laughed. When each wiped tears away with the tips of her fingers, Amanda noticed their gestures were identical.

"We are so pathetic," her mother choked.

"Yes, we are."

Her mom sniffled a few times, gripped the oars and continued rowing. "I know you're worried about Sara."

Amanda took a deep breath. "Of course I am. I have no way to get in touch with her, so I have to assume she's still in custody."

"You've tried her parents?"

"They don't return my calls, and I don't have a phone number for Sara or her brother. I've left messages for Detective Molerno but he won't call me back either."

"I'm so sorry, honey. I wish I could help."

No one can help, Amanda thought bitterly, but she was determined not to cry again.

"Do you want to talk about it?" her mother prompted.

If she only knew. Her mother had given her a perfect opening to come out with the truth about herself and her feelings for Sara, to finally confess she was a lesbian, but she could not do it. She was already too ragged out by the reconciliation with her mother. It wasn't that she lacked the courage; she was simply emotionally drained.

"You asked me to come fishing, but that's not happening, right?" Amanda abruptly changed the subject. She knew for a fact that neither her mother nor Trout enjoyed the sport and claimed to hate killing innocent fish.

"You don't see any rods or worms, do you?" Her mother stopped rowing and lifted the oars into the boat. She removed her baseball cap and ran her fingers through her short white hair. "Let's talk about what happened at Metrolina yesterday. It's upsetting, Mandy. Who would do such a thing to an innocent dove?"

"Someone's sending me a warning, Mom. I tell you, it was that awful June Harris."

She had explained everything to the family last night, but their endless questions had driven her to bed. Instead of the deep sleep she desperately needed, she'd been plagued by bloody nightmares featuring doors opening to the tortured bodies of headless birds. She'd awakened in a cold sweat, and soon after breakfast, been kidnapped by her mother.

"Like I told you, Detective Russell thinks the dove probably died of natural causes. And it's true, a small flock lives up in the rafters. I suppose birds have to die sometime."

"Yes, they do, honey, but they don't end up neatly laid out on your desk. They are seldom carefully beheaded, so of course it was a warning."

"Well, let's hope she got it out of her system." Amanda wanted to believe that June had taken her revenge and would leave her alone in the future. "Detective Russell didn't think it was a big deal."

"So you said. He also wasn't convinced that June Harris had done the deed," her mother persisted. "Didn't he imply that anyone in the building might be motivated to send you that grisly message?"

"Yeah, he also said it could have been one of the Boy Scout Explorers. One of the kids might have found the dead bird, cut off its head and left it as a prank. It's the sort of thing a dumb kid would do."

"Do you believe that?" her mother asked.

"Not for one minute."

"Neither do I." She stretched her long arms, cupped her hands, brought up some cold lake water, and tossed it on Amanda's bare tummy.

Amanda shrieked. "What the hell, Mom?"

Her mother laughed uproariously. "That's my girl! Remember when you were little and I kept trying to interest you in horseback riding?"

Amanda grunted. Her mother had always been an avid horsewoman, but Amanda thought the beasts were hairy, scary and smelly. "Sure. I kept falling off."

"And what did I always say when that happened?"

"Give me a break, Mother." Amanda struggled upright. She found an old bait can, filled it with water and tossed it at her.

She shrieked. "What the hell, Mandy? I didn't mean you had to jump right up and go back to Metrolina today. After all, it's Sunday, a day of rest. Tomorrow will do just fine."

CHAPTER THIRTY-THREE

New keys...

Mama knows best, but Mama wasn't the one who had to get back on the horse. Amanda was gun-shy and more than a little apprehensive about returning to Metrolina. She procrastinated on the way, stopping at a bank—Wells Fargo, of course—to open a personal checking account and deposit the ten thousand dollar check. She stopped at a hardware store to have a duplicate key cut for Jenny Monroe.

She had deliberately dressed in black jeans and T-shirt, hoping the outfit would help her disappear, and when she arrived, she parked on the far side of Building 15 instead of 16. The parking space once removed was isolated, unguarded by the handful of cops still on duty, so maybe no one would notice she was there.

Of course, it was ridiculous to think she could slip in incognito, but it made her feel better, somehow, to try. And in spite of the fact that she knew there would be no trace of the bird body in her booth—Detective Russell had removed and sanitized the mess before she left Saturday afternoon—the image still haunted her.

As she approached her building, Amanda noticed one lone cop stationed at the corner so that he could observe both the alley and the north entrance. She assumed it would be similarly guarded at the south entrance, the Orlandos' end, and wondered how long the police would keep this up. Surely by now the authorities realized the stupid letter was long gone.

All the uniforms seemed to know her. The guy at the corner smiled and waved as she passed, and Amanda decided she was secretly grateful for their continued presence. Truth be told, she was scared witless by everything that had transpired in this cursed building and had begun to wonder if she really wanted to keep renting there.

On the other hand, she'd done well at Metrolina. As she thought about her fat bank balance, she was well aware that time was flying. She had less than one month to come up with the sketches for the sailboat commission and only two weeks to create more small sculpture for the next show. So she had to get busy. Cutting and running was not an option.

From the corner of her eye, she saw that Jack and June Harris were out near their RV, eating lunch at their picnic table. Thank heavens for small favors. At least she would not be immediately accosted by the angry pair. She was, however, snagged by Lucy Monroe, who pulled her inside her booth.

"Glad I caught you, Amanda. I want to tell you something."

Suddenly the new key in her jeans pocket made her feel guilty. Looking around, she noticed Jenny wasn't there. "What's up, Lucy?"

"You know I have the *gift*, right? It came to me in a dream that it was June Harris who put that poor bird on your desk." The pottery woman's plump hands twitched.

"I'd more or less come to that conclusion myself. What about Jack, what's happening with him?" Amanda had already discovered the highly effective gossip network in this place. Everyone knew everyone else's business. Since Lucy Monroe and Jack Harris shared a common pegboard wall, the grapevine should be extra strong at that juncture.

Sure enough, Lucy did not hesitate. "After your tip, that handsome Detective Russell demanded to know what Jack had shipped in those cardboard envelopes you told him about. Luckily, Jack had one of those long receipt tapes from the post office. It listed the destination and insurance value of everything he mailed that day."

"So he's off the hook?" Amanda sincerely hoped the receipt proved Jack was innocent. Then the Harris couple would get off her case.

"Nope, there's a problem," Lucy said gleefully. "Of the five shipped, four went to legitimate customers. They have already been called and have verified that they received antique prints from Jack."

"Wait, how do you know all this, Lucy? Surely Detective Russell doesn't share the results of his investigation with you, and please don't tell me you saw it in a vision."

Lucy's laughter made her ample bosom bounce. "Heavens, no. I hear things." She touched her ear and nodded in the direction of Jack's booth. "When Russell came to report on the first four, he had a question about the fifth addressed to a nameless post office box holder in Pensacola, Florida. The Harrises live in Pensacola all winter, so dollars to doughnuts, that postal box is owned by Jack, by his son Jack Junior, or by some good ole buddy of his."

"So what?"

"So he could have shipped the stolen letter to himself or someone he trusted, then planned to market it later."

"Did someone say dollars to doughnuts?" The man intruded into Lucy's booth. "Being an underpaid and hungry cop, I'd appreciate both the dollars and the doughnuts."

Lucy blushed crimson, while Amanda felt guilty by association. She'd expected to see Detective Russell, not Rick Molerno. Her last experience with the homicide detective, the day he took Sara from the Orlandos' house, had not been cordial.

"Harboring more fugitives today, Ms. Rittenhouse? Or have you and Lucy solved the letter theft?"

Had she been differently oriented, Amanda would have found Molerno attractive. Unlike the dapper Detective Russell, his suit was rumpled, his cheap tie tugged loose from around his muscular neck. His jaw sprouted an afternoon shadow, and his black hair bristled in a buzz cut. He looked like an Italian street fighter.

Lucy struck a defensive pose. "Last I heard, it's not a crime to eavesdrop. Not my fault Detective Russell has a loud voice."

Molerno chuckled. "Well, I'll save you ladies the trouble of putting your ears to the wall by telling you outright. The fifth letter was a dead end. You were correct, Lucy, the P.O. Box belongs to Jack Harris, Jr., and when our counterparts in Florida questioned Junior, he admitted to receiving some posters from his dad. But when pressed, he got hostile and could not produce those posters."

"There you go!" Lucy crowed. "Junior has the stolen letter."

"Inconclusive, my dear Watson." Molerno lifted his dark eyebrows in a pathetic Sherlock Holmes imitation. "Besides, would you entrust something so valuable to the US Mail?"

Amanda and Lucy glanced at one another. Of course not.

"But that's not why I'm here…" Rick Molerno dug into his sagging pocket and brought out three manila coin envelopes. "Detective Russell asked me to give you these keys. They've installed the locks between your booths and your studios." He handed one to Amanda, one to Lucy. "The keys I'm giving both of you are actually duplicates that work the door in Ms. Rittenhouse's Space D, since that's the one you need to use, Lucy. Management is holding a different one for the door in Mrs. Harris's booth, but since June doesn't rent workspace, her pass-through is now firmly locked." He looked meaningfully at Amanda. "In other words, the Harrises no longer have access back there."

Unless, Amanda thought, the Harrises had found Jenny's lost keys and still had access through the alley. She really should tell Molerno about the lost keys, but not in Lucy's presence. She still didn't want to get Jenny in trouble.

As though reading her mind, Molerno spoke again. "I have also asked management to change the locks on the alley doors. They will accomplish this by the weekend, and then our job here will be finished."

So Amanda had wasted her money making a duplicate key for Jenny, but no big deal. She was troubled, however, that soon the police would be gone. After all, there was still a murderer on the loose.

"But neither crime has been solved, Detective," Lucy said. "Does that mean the exhibitors are no longer suspects?"

"Did I say that?" He gave them a silly grin. "We know where to find you, especially *you*, Ms. Rittenhouse. And by the way, I'd like a word with you in private."

Before he tucked the third key envelope into his pocket, Amanda saw Marc Orlando's name written on it.

"As soon as you've finished chatting with Lucy, please meet me down at the café. I'll be waiting."

CHAPTER THIRTY-FOUR

Collective amnesia…

Feeling like a kid being summoned to the principal's office, Amanda said good-bye to Lucy and hurried down the hall. She found Molerno seated in one of the wire Popsicle chairs at the same round table she had briefly shared with Sara. Today, with the café closed and Building 16 in semidarkness, the place had a sad, empty feel. Without the crowds, the only sounds were the doves fluttering near the ceiling and the scraping of furniture being moved in the Thigpen booth across the way.

The detective had removed his jacket and was fingering a pack of cigarettes, clearly trying to decide whether etiquette allowed him to light up in a No Smoking zone. He decided against it and stuffed the pack in his shirt pocket.

Amanda slid nervously into the chair beside him. "How can I help, Detective?"

He laughed, stretched his arms, locked his hands behind his head, and then stared at her. "Well, you can start by telling me how Sara Orlando's fingerprints got on the murder weapon."

Amanda was eager to explain. "She had nothing to do with the murder. It was an unhappy coincidence."

"Yeah, that's what Sara keeps telling me. She says you'll back up her story."

"Oh, yes, I will!" Amanda pointed across the hall to where the Porters were arranging their display. "Mr. Porter will confirm it too. He saw Sara handle the tomahawk early Saturday evening and made her put it down. Don't take my word for it, let's go ask him."

"That was my plan, Ms. Rittenhouse."

They crossed the hall and approached the pair. Again Amanda was amazed at how different the couple seemed. Maribelle no longer gave off her old maid schoolteacher vibe, while Carlson seemed less ineffectual, more assertive. More than that, they seemed happy together, giggling like newlyweds.

"Can we help you?" Maribelle looked up from her task of sewing a torn pocket on a vintage army uniform that smelled of mothballs.

"Come in, Detective Molerno." Carlson was equally cordial as he paused over a box of rusty old pistols which reeked of oil. "These are from World War I, mostly Brownings, but also a few Colts. With a little TLC, they will all be serviceable again."

Molerno was distracted by the guns. "You mean people actually buy these and fire them?" He picked up one Amanda thought she recognized from the old cowboy movies. "Is this a Colt .45?"

"You bet. Manufactured in 1898, sweet little six-shooter."

Amanda hung back. She knew better than to touch a weapon in this booth. "How is Mr. Thigpen? Is he home from the hospital yet?"

Carlson Porter's sunny attitude turned stormy. He glanced at his wife, who frowned and looked up from her sewing. "As Maribelle will tell you, Michael is home, but he won't be permitted to work for several months."

"And we're getting along fine without him," Maribelle added testily.

Amanda decided they were doing more than getting along; they were thriving. In the short time she'd observed this family's dynamic, it was obvious that Mr. Thigpen was the Alpha dog, a very overbearing boss.

"I was sorry to read about the insurance money," she said. "I understand it doesn't begin to cover the value of the stolen letter."

Porter glared at her. "I don't see how that's any of your business, young lady. My brother-in-law was foolish not to insure it for more, but that's water under the bridge now."

Amanda backed up another pace. The little man was creepy, like a small, unpredictable dog who looked cute until he jumped up and bit you. And he was growing more impatient by the minute.

"What do you want, Detective?" he snapped.

Molerno got right to the point, relating how both Amanda and Sara had explained Sara's prints on the SOG tactical tomahawk. He did a good job, but Porter was unimpressed.

He shook his head. "No, I do not remember such an incident. I'm afraid these girls are mistaken."

Amanda was floored. "Of course you remember, Mr. Porter. Sara picked up the tomahawk, then you came over and got mad at her. You were wearing a sailor suit costume and white gloves. You put the tomahawk back on display on a red silk scarf."

"It never happened, Detective," Porter declared. "I appreciate how Miss Orlando might want to exonerate herself of this terrible crime…" He frowned at Amanda. "And how a good friend might like to support her, but I can't be party to this preposterous story."

Amanda could have killed Porter on the spot. She knew damned well the man remembered. And then Maribelle stepped forward like a gawky giraffe.

"I was there too, Detective," Maribelle said. "If there had been such a disturbance, I would have noticed. My husband is telling the truth. It never happened."

Make that a double homicide. Amanda wanted to kill them both. Anger pulsed in her temples and heat rushed to her face.

Somehow, she managed to hold her tongue, but murderous looks passed between them.

"Thank you for your time, folks," Molerno said mildly as he took firm hold of Amanda's elbow and steered her away. "I'll get back to you if I have any more questions."

As soon as they were out of earshot, Amanda exploded. "They're lying! What's wrong with them? I know they remember!"

He guided her outside the south door and they stood side by side in the late afternoon sun. "The other exhibitors have told me how Mr. Thigpen and the Porters wore those white gloves. Everyone thought it was a snobbish affectation."

"The gloves also kept their fingerprints off the weapon. In fact, I bet they polished their special pieces before the show so that there were no fingerprints until Sara's." Amanda was livid.

But Molerno remained calm. "I suspect you're right, Ms. Rittenhouse, because Sara's were the only prints on the tomahawk."

"Is that good, or bad for Sara?"

He thought about it. "That depends. If your story is true, it means that any killer other than Sara had to have worn gloves to keep their fingerprints off hers. If the Porter story is true, we're back to square one, and Sara is screwed."

"But the Porters are lying. Can't you see that?"

"A case of collective amnesia?" Molerno chuckled and lit a cigarette. Here in the open air, he no longer had to worry about political correctness.

Amanda wasn't sure what to make of him. "Are you saying you believe Sara is innocent?"

"Let's just say I'm not convinced she is guilty. That's why I cut her loose." He smiled slyly at Amanda. "We still have a boatload of evidence against her, especially considering that fistfight she had with Ben in the parking lot..."

"But?" Amanda found herself daring to hope.

"But we're conducting interviews with Dr. Orlando's coworkers to get a take on her relationship with Ben."

"And?"

"And it's a mixed bag. The professional staff claims Sara would never resort to murder, but they all admit Ben Marsh had been stalking her. Those who side with Ben—mostly parolees and addicts who have an ax to grind with Dr. Orlando—say she's a stone-cold bitch for rejecting him."

"And what do you think, Detective?"

He ground the cigarette butt under the toe of his shoe. "I think the jury's still out."

CHAPTER THIRTY-FIVE

Taking inventory...

As soon as Molerno dismissed her, Amanda rushed toward her own booth. Ignoring the angry stares of Carlson and Maribelle Porter, she shoved past Jack and June Harris, who seemed determined to confront her as she ducked under her blue tarp. She quickly tested the new key, and then passed into her workspace. When she locked that door behind her, she suddenly appreciated the fact that now no one could barge in and hassle her.

Taking a deep breath, she sank onto a plastic folding chair she'd hauled up from Florida and took stock of her fragile emotions. While she breathed in, then out, Amanda gazed at her pile of welding equipment stacked in one corner, at the Monroe pottery wheel and kiln, at Marc's stash of old wood flooring and various architectural salvage, and collected her thoughts. The studio smelled of damp clay, linseed oil and dust.

Oddly, it also smelled of hope. Not because those odors were comfortingly familiar from warehouse studios where she'd worked in the past, but because of what Detective Molerno had just said: *I cut her loose.* So Sara wasn't suffering in some awful jail. She was free—at least for the moment.

The thought lifted her spirits and moved her to action. So what if half her fellow exhibitors hated her guts? She could live with that. Yesterday Metrolina had seemed a gloomy, foreboding place, causing her to wonder if she could break her lease. But now everything had changed.

Amanda got up, turned on the lights and got busy with the inventory she'd tried to accomplish since Saturday. She unpacked a box including her welding clothes: face shield with adjustable headband, leather gloves, work apron, leather jacket, high-top shoes and safety glasses. If Sara saw her in this getup, would she be impressed?

The next box included her tools: chipping hammer, wire brush, vice-grips and clamps, anvil, tongs, long-handled pliers. Simply handling these items was a joy, and she imagined the art she would create—maybe even a special piece for Sara's apartment, as she had requested.

She had a few welding rods on hand which were used to make the strong seams in her metal constructions, but she'd need to buy more. Finally, she carefully unpacked her portable oxygen/acetylene outfit on wheels. She inspected the cylinder, valves, gauges and hose. The system had cost Amanda a small fortune, but in light of the lucrative Wells Fargo commission, it was worth every penny. She kept her cutting torch and welding tips in a special case, and figured she'd easily find a shop to supply her with gas. So she was all set.

But her head was spinning. Weaving in and out of the tapestry of designs she was mentally composing were the nagging threads of worry, all about Sara. It made it hard to concentrate. Where was Sara now? With Lena, or at home in her balcony hidey-hole?

Most important, how could she get in touch with her? She didn't have Sara's phone number. Suddenly she realized she was pacing and directed that movement south, toward Marc's studio. If only he were there, perhaps he'd give her the number? Along the way, just for fun, Amanda quietly tested the door into June Harris's booth. It was firmly locked. She smiled in satisfaction.

But when she tried Marc's door, it too was locked. *Damn!*
Putting her ear to it, she heard only silence. When the hell
would Marc put in an appearance? Frustrated, Amanda sat
down on an old window seat much like the one that had served
as Ben Marsh's coffin.

Shivering involuntarily, she took out her cell phone, found
the number for Metrolina Main Office among her contacts,
and impulsively dialed. When the lease manager answered, she
introduced herself and asked for Marc's number. Miraculously,
the man complied.

Oh my God! She quickly entered it into her phone and began
working up the courage to dial. In the meantime, her phone
began playing "Disco Inferno," her personal ringtone. The
sound made her leap like Stephen Curry on a jumpshot.

"Hello?" She didn't recognize the caller ID.

"Hi, Amanda, it's Sara. Thank God I got you!"

Amanda immediately sat down again. "Sara, I've been trying
to reach you too. Are you okay?"

"I just got a call from Detective Molerno. He told me what
happened with you and the Porters. Jesus, Amanda, I'm so
sorry!"

Sara sounded breathless and frightened. "No, I'm the one
who's sorry. I can't believe those shits wouldn't back up our
story."

"I know, but I sense Molerno thinks they're lying. And I
want to thank you for trying, Amanda. In person."

Amanda nearly slid off the window seat. "You want to see
me? When?"

As Sara explained that she was still living in the building
behind her parents' house, and that she wanted to see her as
soon as possible, Amanda was on her feet, running back toward
the door to her booth so she could leave immediately.

"I'll be right there!" she promised Sara.

None of the other exhibitors approached her on the way
out, but the guard at the north exit searched her purse, causing
her to wriggle with impatience. When he finally let her go, she
was momentarily disoriented because she could not find her car.

But then she remembered. She had parked in the alley behind Building 15, one door down, hoping to sneak into Metrolina unnoticed. Walking fast in the right direction, Amanda was surprised to see that the sun was setting, and she hoped she'd find her way to the Orlandos' house in the near darkness.

As soon as she rounded the corner and saw Moby, Amanda realized something was terribly wrong. And when she got close, the enormity of the problem brought tears of anger to her eyes. Her big white van seemed to be sinking into the alley, and when she rounded it, she saw that all four tires had been slashed. Moby Dyke was resting on her rims.

Oh God damn! She unlocked the driver's side, slid in, and lay her forehead on the steering wheel. Who would do such a thing? She came up with quite a few likely suspects. She'd tell the cop, but that wouldn't help her one little bit when all she wanted was to get to Sara. She'd have to call and cancel.

CHAPTER THIRTY-SIX

Comfort zone...

"You should have called me. I would have picked you up," Trout told her. He was still miffed because last night Amanda had taken a cab all the way from Charlotte to Mooresville.

"I didn't want to bother anyone. Besides, I can afford it."

"Yeah, I know, that big advance on your commission is burning a hole in your pocket, so maybe you'd like to spend some of it right here at home?"

Amanda didn't know what Trout had up his sleeve, but after feeding her a huge lunch, he had bundled her into his old Ford pickup and driven her to his store, Trout's Place, on River Highway. The combination gas station, general store and auto repair shop had been in business forever. And today Trout had insisted that Amanda visit the auto repair shop.

"When do you think Hoke will be back with my van?" she asked. It wasn't that she didn't appreciate that Trout had sent two of his employees, along with four new tires, down to Metrolina to repair Moby. But she was burning with impatience to see Sara.

"I reckon they'll be back by five. Just count yourself lucky to have family in the auto repair business."

"You must let me pay you, Trout." She squeezed his arm as he led her into a dark garage.

"Cut it out, moneybags. You're as bad as your mama. She can't accept any favor without a fight."

Lest she again be compared to her mother, she reluctantly accepted the free tires and service call.

"But why are we here?" She blinked twice when Trout turned on the lights and saw an abandoned service bay with a lift, as well as shelves holding everything from motor oil to a muffler display. The concrete floors were stained from years of dripping automotive fuels, and the room stank of grease and rubber.

Trout smiled. "We haven't used this part of the garage in years, so I intend to make you an offer you can't refuse."

She shifted from foot to foot and wished he would go away so she could call Sara. Last night Sara had been hysterical after Amanda told her about the dead bird and slashed tires, and she'd claimed to be worried about Amanda's safety. Diana, Trout and Ginny had also been way beyond upset, and were getting downright pushy about how Amanda should conduct her life. She strongly suspected today's outing had something to do with her family's concerns.

"Your mom and I have decided it's not safe for you to be working alone at Metrolina, especially once you get started on that big piece for the bank," Trout said.

She started to protest, but Trout held up both hands.

"Now please hear me out, Mandy Bear. I've been listening to your description of what you're planning to build, and this garage is where you need to build it." He gestured at the lift. "I have everything you need in here. You said the commission will be upward of twelve feet tall, so it'll be mighty heavy. We can rig a framework on the lift, and you can work at any height you choose." He pointed to the high windows surrounding the room. "You'll have plenty of sunlight so you can see what you're doing, and this space was used for a welding shop for years."

Amanda quickly saw the merit in Trout's ideas. She'd not only be safe here, but also only five minutes from home. "But I've already paid for my workspace at Metrolina."

"So break your lease. Besides, Mandy, auto parts are my stock-n'-trade. I know all the junkyards and the acetylene providers. You're my second daughter, right? So why not let me help you?"

Trout's argument made sense, and Amanda was deeply moved by his attention. Obviously he'd been listening to her design plans and cared, wanted to be part of the whole process.

"So how much will you charge me for this sorry old garage?"

He laughed. "Since you're rich, it won't be free, but I promise you'll get the family discount."

She submitted to his bone-crushing hug, knowing full well that in Trout's mind, the hug equaled a handshake. Amanda hated her fear, her nightmares, and the way the tire slashing had reduced her to a trembling little girl. She'd never thought of herself as a coward. After all, one had to be a tiny bit brave to be gay in a straight world. But she'd never come out to her mother, nor to anyone else whose opinion critically mattered. So here she was prepared to shelter in the safe haven of a father figure who called her Mandy Bear and called his real daughter Ginny Bean. What was she, six years old?

She pulled away, and Trout frowned.

"Look, Mandy, you don't have to decide today. It's just an idea, but it's your decision. Just remember, it would make your mother and me real happy."

"Thanks, Trout, I promise to think about it very seriously."

"That's all I ask." He winked, and then they both walked back outside to the sunshine. As they stood side by side watching the traffic flow on River Highway, Amanda spotted Moby driving toward them on four new rubber paws.

"Look, Trout, they got my van fixed!"

"Sure they did."

He walked forward to greet his best friend, Hoke Bodine. As Hoke climbed from her van's large belly, she saw he was as thin and black as Moby was fat and white, a stunning image for the right artist.

"Hey buddy," Trout said. "You're just in time for dinner— fried chicken and biscuits down by the lake. Why don't you come home with Mandy and me?"

"Hey, man, you don't need to ask twice. Of course I'll come."

"Uh, no, thanks," Amanda said quickly, before they could change her mind and pull her deeper into that seductive comfort zone. "I need to go now, sorry."

Trout's smile drooped. "Where are you going?"

"To see a friend. I was on my way there last evening before all this happened." She nodded at Moby.

"You're goin' back to Charlotte?" Hoke asked incredulously. She nodded.

"But I just got back from there." Hoke sounded as though he thought the concept was nonsensical.

She shrugged, then looked apologetically at Trout. She could tell he was struggling mightily to keep his mouth shut and not argue with her. Trout's silence was a vote of confidence, allowing Amanda to assert her adulthood.

She hoped she could live up to that high ideal. As she climbed into Moby and dialed Sara's number, she saw Trout and Hoke standing side by side in her rearview mirror. Each man had his hand lifted to his forehead, shielding his vision as he looked into the sun, watching her.

"Hi Sara," she said into the phone. "Do you want to try again?"

CHAPTER THIRTY-SEVEN

It's complicated...

It was too late to fret about her attire: old jeans shorts, wrinkled red T-shirt, worn flip-flops. At least she'd shaved her legs, which were tan thanks to years in Florida and a summer at the lake. Besides, Sara had said "Come as you are." She had also said that Amanda should bypass the Orlando house and come straight to the metal building. She'd leave the door open and have supper waiting.

All well and good. Very good, in fact. But that didn't ease her nervous anxiety as she drove past the house and saw Juan and Sofia through the lighted kitchen window. They were standing near the stove, likely discussing their dinner menu, hopefully oblivious to the fact that an unwelcome interloper was sneaking onto their property.

Amanda's hands were sweating as she parked on the far side of the building and slipped into the warehouse. It wasn't like this was a date, or anything like it. No doubt Sara just wanted to talk about the murder. Which was unpleasant enough, but not nearly as scary as discussing more personal matters.

"Come on up!" Sara called from the top of the stairs.

She stood at the banister, silhouetted by the strong backlight of the sunset blazing through the far window. With each step, Amanda's heartbeat accelerated. She was coming to dinner empty-handed, socially inept, and awkward as a besotted schoolgirl. But when she reached the landing, Sara smiled and pulled her into her arms.

"I'm so glad you came, Amanda," she whispered against her ear.

Amanda was stunned, overwhelmed, her body stiff with surprise as Sara held her. In her dreams, she had imagined how Sara would feel and how they would fit together—she so tall, Sara so small. No problem, it was easy. Sara's generous breasts tucked under Amanda's smaller ones. The fresh scent of Sara's soft hair nestled into the tender spot beneath her chin. Perfect, really.

But all too soon it was over. Sara pulled away, then held her at arm's length. "You look good," she said.

"So do you," Amanda mumbled self-consciously. "Your black eye's almost better."

Sara's hearty laugh enveloped her. "Right, so now that I look less like a street thug, I won't terrify my patients."

She took Amanda's hand and led her into the room. "I took two weeks' vacation from work. Being a murder suspect doesn't inspire confidence in folks with major problems of their own. I heard the police have been asking questions down at the office, and I didn't want to be there."

"Detective Molerno told me about that. I'm so sorry."

She let go of Amanda's hand and faced her. "It's been a nightmare for all of us, which is precisely why I don't want to talk about it tonight. Not one word about the theft or the murder. Do we have a deal?"

Amanda gulped. So they'd be talking about scary personal matters after all. "Deal. I promise not to discuss any of it."

"Very good. That means we can actually enjoy a meal together this time." Sara moved to a counter and opened two large white bags. "Thai takeout okay with you?"

"Very okay. I love it."

The small table near the window was set for two, with wineglasses and a stubby candle in a Ball jar. The burning candle could not yet compete with the amazing blue and pink sunset strutting its stuff above the empty fields outside. Amanda began to relax, until she realized this was maybe a date after all.

"I bought pineapple gai pan, made with stir-fried chicken, snow peas, bamboo shoots, carrots, baby onions and pineapple chunks in a sweet and sour wine sauce."

"Yummy." Amanda wasn't sure how close to move toward Sara as she opened the boxes.

"This one's called Sea of Love..." Sara winked. "With stir-fried calamari, shrimp, scallops and herbs in a spicy sauce."

"Even better."

It seemed Sara was slightly nervous too as she recited the menu. Amanda tried not to remember how a dish identical to Sea of Love had been Rachel's favorite. Just as she was working up the courage to move in and peek over Sara's shoulder, Sara's cell phone rang.

"Damn it!" She rolled her eyes and checked her caller ID. "It's Mama. I better answer."

Amanda couldn't help overhearing part of the conversation. It wasn't pretty.

"Sorry," Sara muttered as she ended the call. "They saw you drive in and wanted to know why you're here. As you heard, I told her it was none of their business. They'll leave us alone now."

Amanda sighed. "I understand. It's not easy living with your parents. I'm in the same boat right now."

As Sara filled the plates and nuked them in the microwave, she handed Amanda a bottle of white Zinfandel and a corkscrew. In the meantime, Amanda explained the bare bones of her move from Florida to Mooresville, adding that she hoped that living cheek by jowl with her mother and Trout was only temporary.

By the time they sat down to the sumptuous meal, Amanda sensed they were easier with one another, although the electricity sparking between them was undeniable.

"To us." Sara proposed the toast.

"Yes, to us." Amanda blushed as they touched glasses, and then began to eat.

Somehow the silence, punctuated by little grunts of approval for the food, was not intimidating. As the room retreated into darkness, the single candle illuminated Sara's dramatic coloring—rosy cheeks and lips—an emerald-green blouse brought out her eyes, and the wine warmed them.

"I'm surprised you didn't go back to Lena's," Amanda said, still thinking about the problem of living with parents.

Sara thought about it as she pushed a lone chunk of pineapple around on her otherwise empty plate. "I think I told you that Lena and I have some unresolved issues."

Amanda was dying to hear more, but dared not press too hard. "It seems like Lena's jealous of Marc, like maybe she doesn't want to share you with him?"

The comment made Sara hiccup with uncontrollable laughter. When the convulsions subsided, she said, "You've got that ass-backward, my friend. Lena doesn't want to share Marc with me."

"I don't understand."

"I met Lena when she was dating my brother. When he dropped her to move on to yet another girlfriend, she was devastated. I think she invited me to be her housemate just so she'd have a lifeline to Marc, but it hasn't worked out that way. She loves him, but she claims to hate him, and I'm stuck somewhere in the middle to remind Lena that Marc's close with me, not her."

"That's complicated." As Amanda absorbed the news and realized Lena was straight, she wondered: what did that say about Sara?

"No shit, it's complicated. I'm a shrink, and I can't sort it out. And quite frankly, I'm tired of trying." She ate the lonely pineapple, then stared at Amanda. "But I do know one thing, Amanda. I owe you an apology."

With no idea what would come out next, Amanda braced herself. Obviously Sara was experiencing some discomfort as she tried to find the right words.

"Last time you were here, before we were so rudely interrupted by Detective Molerno, you very bravely told me something about yourself…" Finally Sara looked unflinchingly into Amanda's eyes. "You said that you were not attracted to any men, that you much preferred women…"

Amanda held her breath.

"Well, if I'd had the courage or the time," Sara continued, "I would have told you that I'm a member of your club, Amanda. I'm a lesbian. I should have said it then, and I'm sorry."

Coming out is never easy. Paradoxically, it can be even harder saying it to someone you really care about, someone with whom you might want a relationship. Eventually Amanda exhaled and reached across the table for Sara's hand. "It's all good," she told her.

She looked out the window and saw the first stars hung in the darkening sky. She smelled the hot wax and heard soft music playing in the background. She noticed Sara's futon had been opened into a bed, with four pillows neatly stacked at one end.

"I don't do relationships though," Sara warned, softening the words with a smile. "I'm not good at commitment."

At that point, Amanda didn't care, even though her adult life so far had been all about one relationship, one commitment. Maybe Sara would think she was the epitome of the lesbian stereotype—the girl who has one successful date, then calls the moving van to move in with her lover. Well, Amanda had been that girl, hadn't she?

"I get it, Sara," she said slowly. "You're not looking for rings and wedding bells."

"Not even if I could!" Sara stood up and walked behind Amanda's chair. She leaned over and kissed the back of her neck, then brought her lips around to find Amanda's mouth.

Amanda swiveled to meet the kiss full on. As lips brushed and lingered, she was glad she was seated, or her knees would have buckled. Clearly Sara knew what she was doing, playing her like a virtuoso, applying just enough pressure so that Amanda's body begged for more. When Sara's teasing tongue outlined her lips, then plunged between them, the jolt of desire sent lightning down her spine to her loins. As Sara's rhythmic dance continued, Amanda believed she would either burn, or melt, but then Sara paused.

She gently helped Amanda to stand on shaky legs, and then searched her eyes. "Wait, Amanda, we need to make a decision. Should I make coffee, or skip it and go straight to bed?"

By the time Amanda caught her breath, she'd made her decision. "Skip the coffee, but I'll have to call my mom and ask if I can sleep over."

They both laughed.

CHAPTER THIRTY-EIGHT

Mixed signals…

She did not awaken to the homey sizzle of bacon on the stove, nor the smell of fresh brewing coffee—like heroines in romance novels are supposed to do—but rather to the harsh clatter of metal on metal and men laughing directly below their bed. Before she could scream, Sara was on top of her, one hand firmly sealing her mouth.

"It's okay," Sara whispered. "It's the landscape crew loading their trucks. They'll be gone soon."

Amanda was not convinced. In fact, she had never felt so exposed.

"Stay calm. The guys know I'm living up here, and they won't come up. They wouldn't dare." Sara giggled and pulled the sheet over their heads. "If I take my hand away, will you promise not to scream?"

Amanda nodded vigorously, accepting a kiss in replacement of the hand, and then she froze until the ordeal was over, until the last man left the building. She didn't know whether to laugh or cry when they finally emerged from their tent.

"Well, that was fun," she gasped.

"It was, wasn't it?" Sara offered a devilish grin as she sat on the edge of the bed, her beautiful body glowing in the early morning light.

"Not my idea of a good time." Amanda peevishly snatched up her clothes, which lay in a ruined heap beside the futon, and stomped toward the shower. Glancing back over her shoulder, she saw Sara standing there, looking confused.

Too bad.

As warm water pulsed over her skin, Amanda realized several things. Every muscle in her body ached from their acrobatic lovemaking, but it was a good ache. Rachel and she had never behaved with such wild abandon. Instead, their coupling had always been serious, intense, and even tearful with emotion. Sara was playful, prone to laughing with each new delight, and Amanda was amazed by the contrast.

As she relived their antics of a few minutes ago, the panic under the sheet, suddenly she was laughing too. Maybe she had better get with the program and grow a sense of humor.

She found she was actually whistling when she emerged, holding her dirty clothes in her hands, clad only in one of Sara's short T-shirts that barely covered her decently. Her bare feet left moist footprints on the hardwood as she plodded toward the homey sizzle of bacon and the smell of fresh brewing coffee she'd expected all along.

"Feeling better?" Sara called cheerfully.

"Smells good. I guess you're planning to feed me again."

"So it would seem, but you better put your shorts on before I get completely distracted." Sara broke some eggs into a frying pan. "And you'll have to eat and run, I'm afraid."

"Why? You have someplace better to be?" Amanda decided Sara looked gorgeous even in her ratty terrycloth robe and the fuzzy pink slippers she'd worn the first time Amanda visited.

"There's no place better than being here with you, Amanda, but alas, I promised my brother I'd help him haul a load of bricks today."

Marc again. Hauling bricks beat a morning with her? "Are you serious?" She pulled on her shorts.

"A promise is a promise," Sara said lightly. "I'm really sorry."

Was she? As Amanda sat down to breakfast across from Sara, a painful lump filled her throat as she tried to gauge Sara's sincerity. Had this been a one-night stand? After all, Sara had said upfront she wasn't into relationships, or commitment. But after the magical hours they'd just shared, when in spite of the shower Amanda still felt this woman's scent imprinted on her skin, how could it be over?

"I really am sorry," Sara repeated. "But Marc's all set to deliver this load to Metrolina tomorrow, and he couldn't find anyone else to help him. Besides..." She touched Amanda's thigh under the table. "The exercise will do me good, work out the kinks."

"You call what ails us *kinks*?"

"*Kinky*, maybe?" Sara's infectious laugh echoed in the steel building, causing Amanda to believe she had better grow that sense of humor fast, because this woman's comedy was leaving her in the dust.

The coffee tasted bitter on her tongue, and she wasn't able to finish her meal. Their imminent separation did not affect Sara's appetite at all. Indeed, she radiated a kind of joy that Amanda did not understand. Did she dare hope that she, Amanda, had inspired the good mood? The focused twinkle in Sara's green eyes did not discourage this hope, but coward that she was, Amanda didn't trust it.

When Sara excused herself to dress, Amanda washed the dishes and discovered their proper places in the cupboards. While she listened to Sara singing in the shower, she admitted she'd never been good at mixed signals. And by the time her lover emerged, stunning in old khakis, a striped blouse, and sneaks sprinkled with silly glitter, Amanda was in turmoil.

"When will I see you again?" she blurted.

Sara crossed the room and pulled her into her arms. "Soon, I hope. Unless they lock me up and throw away the keys." She gave Amanda a lingering kiss. "And speaking of keys, take this and lock up when you go. For future reference, I hide it under the flowerpot outside the door."

And then she was gone, scampering down the stairs without a backward glance.

CHAPTER THIRTY-NINE

A new life...

The drive to Mooresville passed in a blur as Amanda second-guessed herself. In spite of the humming muscles and nerve endings that told her something extraordinary had happened to her body, the hours spent with Sara took on the aspect of a surreal dream. Had it really happened? And what did it mean?

Everything else had evaporated from her brain. She hadn't thought once about the theft, the murder, or the endless questions her mother would ask about her night spent away from home. Indeed, she couldn't concentrate at all as she sped up the interstate. When she arrived at the lake cottage in one piece, she counted it as a major miracle.

The haze of unreality persisted as she parked, walked toward the screened-in porch, and saw Ginny standing there. No, not standing, but rather jumping like a crazed jack-in-the-box. Ginny gestured wildly, mouthing a secret message Amanda couldn't understand. But when Ginny pointed at the extra car parked in their driveway, Amanda tumbled back to earth with the impact of a meteor strike.

The familiar BMW had Florida plates.

"Oh my God!" Ginny intoned as Amanda peeked into the house.

Her mother, Trout, and even little Lissa, home from summer camp, were sitting around the dining room table with the stranger, chatting together like they'd known her all their lives.

Ginny pulled Amanda aside for a stage whisper. "She's been here for an hour, and our parents are eating it up. Rachel billed herself as your best friend in all the world."

"Why didn't you call and warn me?"

"Damn it, Amanda, I tried. I called and called, left a voice message, but you never responded."

"That's impossible." Or was it? She reached into the front pocket of her jeans, but her cell phone was gone. Shit! She'd left it at Sara's. Amanda pictured it sitting dead center on the black lacquer table near the futon, black on black. Out of sight, out of mind.

"Where were you, anyway?" Ginny demanded, and then her mouth dropped open. "Please don't tell me you spent the night with Rachel! She said she had a motel right here in town. How could you?"

"I didn't. You're crazy!"

"Then where the hell were you?"

"None of your business."

"Oh God, you were with Sara!"

Ginny couldn't let it go, but Amanda wasn't strong enough to explain. She pushed her aside and moved into the house.

By then Amanda was certain she was living a dream, or maybe a nightmare. As she approached the table, Rachel's eyes never left her face. She saw immediately that her ex-lover had aged appreciably in the month or so they'd been apart. She was still heartbreakingly beautiful. Her black hair was streaked with more gray and her intense dark eyes were tired, but her smile was engaging.

"What are you doing here?" Amanda demanded without ceremony.

"Rachel is having a one-woman show of her paintings in Atlanta, so she came on up here to see you," her mother explained enthusiastically.

"And she brought you a load of stuff you left behind." Trout indicated a large cardboard box in the corner.

"Look, Rachel gave me this pirate ship from Disney World." Even Lissa had benefitted from the impromptu visit.

"Oh." Amanda was shell-shocked.

Luckily, Rachel took the initiative, climbing gracefully to her feet. "It's a beautiful day, Amanda, why don't we go down to the lake? We can catch up on everything while we watch the water."

"Yeah, sure." What could she say?

She obediently followed Rachel onto the deck, down the stairs, and straight out to the gazebo. They sat across from one another at the picnic table, and for a long time simply listened to the waves lapping at the shore.

"What do you want, Rach?" Amanda was afraid to look at her lest she fall prey to her seductive spell. At the same time she was too tired to mince words.

Rachel hesitated. "I'm excited about my show in Atlanta. It features my new abstract landscapes you saw before. I was hoping you could join me there for a few days."

Amanda did not hesitate. "I'm happy for you, but now is not a good time."

"Yes, your mother told me about the big commission you landed from Wells Fargo. That's amazing, Amanda, I'm really proud of you."

"Thanks, Rach, but it scares me some. They want drawings."

Her ex laughed and took her hand, forcing Amanda to meet her eyes. "Oh, yes, I remember that sketching isn't your forte. You've always been a hands-on kind of gal. Long as I've known you, you've preferred to assemble all your odds n' ends and let the materials dictate the finished piece. Am I right?"

Amanda nodded. "But this time I need to plan first and come up with something convincing on paper."

"Then it's a good thing I brought your stuff. Your stack of drawing tablets is in that box, and all your pencils."

Amanda had forgotten all about them. "What else did I leave behind?"

A cloud passed over the sun, and Rachel put on her serious face. "You may not want to hear this, and I know you hate guns, but I brought that little Raven pistol I purchased for you, and I'm glad I did."

"I don't want it, Rach."

Back in Sarasota, Rachel had decided that Amanda needed protection. At the time, she'd been living in a rough part of town, taking night classes at the Ringling School of Art. Rachel insisted the "Saturday Night Special," a .25 caliber automatic that fit in the palm of her hand, would keep her safe. She'd forced her to visit a firing range until Amanda had become a decent shot, made her buy a concealed carry license, and in the process made Amanda paranoid about her neighborhood.

Thinking back, the damned gun had been a major factor propelling Amanda to move in with Rachel. Once in Towles Court, she had put the pistol away and tried to forget it ever existed.

"Take the gun back to Sarasota, I don't want it," she repeated.

"No, I'm leaving it with you, Amanda. Your mother told me about the ghastly murder down at that place where you work. I'm so sorry you had to experience that unpleasantness, but it proves you need to carry the Raven with you each time you go there."

Amanda gently removed her hand from Rachel's and studied the older woman. She already knew she couldn't win an argument with her, but for the first time she also realized how much Rachel had controlled every aspect of her life. Yes, Rachel had mentored her, sheltered her, loved her. But in the process, Amanda had lost her own identity.

As they sat there, little Lissa and Ursie ran down to the water's edge. Lissa launched her new pirate ship and Ursie barked as it sailed back and forth, bobbing on the frothy waves. Her mother, Trout and Ginny appeared with cups of coffee and sat on the deck. No doubt they were curious, keeping an eye on the visit of Amanda with her "best friend."

"Why did you really come?" Amanda asked gently.

Rachel sighed. She again tried to capture Amanda's hand, but Amanda moved away.

"Okay, I made a mistake, Amanda," her ex said slowly. "I never should have let you go. I miss you, I love you, and I want you back."

Amanda caught her breath. How many times had she dreamed of Rachel uttering those exact words? She knew full well how hard it was for her to admit such a mistake, and each syllable broke Amanda's heart.

"What about Candy?" Amanda whispered.

"I asked her to leave. She was never right for me, and I'm sure I was wrong for her. Bottom line? She wasn't you, Amanda."

Amanda was almost sorry for Candy. She pictured her gathering up all her sentimental watercolor greeting cards and being tossed out on the street.

"I'm sorry it didn't work out for you."

"Me too, but it woke me up, Amanda. I understood what I had lost."

This was the moment of truth, Amanda's opportunity to change course and take back what she once thought she wanted above all else. But when she looked out at Lissa playing, at her mother, Trout and Ginny on the deck, she saw a family she'd never dared hope to have. This wasn't even about Sara; it was about them.

"I wish I could say yes, Rach, but I can't. I have a new life here, and I like it very much."

"You've found someone else!" Rachel looked devastated.

"Even if that were true, it's not the issue. I really am sorry." Amanda got to her feet and walked back toward the house. Rachel followed, but Amanda firmly directed her back toward her BMW.

"It's best we say goodbye here and now, Rachel. I wish you nothing but happiness."

With that, Amanda turned and walked away.

CHAPTER FORTY

Problematic possessions…

Amanda didn't know what scared her the most—the sketch pads, the love letters, or the gun. Unable to sleep, she had unpacked the box Rachel left while the rest of the household slept. With only a sleepy-eyed Ursie to keep her company, Amanda lifted out old flip-flops, almost forgotten souvenirs collected in her travels, a few favorite shells—items deliberately abandoned. But three of the problematic possessions were in a different league altogether.

The drawing pads represented what Rachel had said: sketching was not her forte. Even in art school, the fundamentals of drawing, perspective and design had eluded her. She was always impatient to move on to the finished product, to assemble her bumpers, gears, tailpipes, hubcaps and other raw materials and start welding. This approach had yielded sculpture admired by both the public and her professors, but left Amanda feeling sheepishly inadequate when it came to the basics.

Now she had a job to do which required her to sharpen her pencils and swallow her inferiority complex. So to that end, with the moon high in the sky and Ginny snoring in the room next door, she put her pads and pencils aside to take to Metrolina the next day.

The stack of love letters she'd written to Rachel had never been perfumed, nor had they been preserved by her lover banded with a ribbon. Instead, Rachel had saved them in a canvas Trader Joe's tote bag, tossed in without regard for chronological order. But Amanda believed they had been treasured all the same.

Why hadn't she saved Rachel's letters, and why had Rachel returned these to her? To prove she had valued Amanda's love, or to reassure Amanda that the letters would never fall into the wrong hands? It was now up to her to decide their fate— preserve, or destroy?

These questions left Amanda crazy with guilt and overcome by memories. The letters were part of her past and also the bridge from her past to her future. She had just banished Rachel, just slept with Sara, not knowing where that relationship would lead, and now she felt stranded midway on that bridge. So she hid the Trader Joe's bag away to deal with later.

That left the gun as the most problematic leg of the triangle. Amanda lifted the little Raven MP-25 from its box and fingered its pearl grip. The magazine held six bullets, plus one in the chamber. Her shooting instructor had assured her all those years ago that while the gun wouldn't punch holes through steel walls, it was very accurate and would get the job done.

She despised all weapons designed to inflict harm on fellow human beings, but she remembered the dead bird, the slashed tires, and the debilitating fear she'd experienced the last time she entered Metrolina. She didn't know if her license to carry a concealed weapon was transferrable to North Carolina, but she was sure she needed to register it in her new state.

In spite of these reservations, Amanda inserted a magazine, pulled up the safety, and tucked the pistol into her purse. Only then, with the moon sharing space with the sunrise, did she climb into bed, invite Ursie to jump up beside her, and pray for a few hours of sleep.

CHAPTER FORTY-ONE

Egg on the sidewalk...

If she broke an egg on the sidewalk, Amanda believed it would fry into breakfast in no time flat. She was sweating as she approached the north entrance, but not just because of the heat. Expecting to be searched, she'd slipped the pistol into her bikini undies under baggy shorts. Definitely uncomfortable, but the guard on duty would have to give her a very personal pat down to find it, and so far, none of the guys had had the nerve.

"Hi there, Amanda!"

As soon as she heard the friendly voice, her blood pressure dropped closer to normal, because Sergeant Ronald Jacobs would never grope her.

"Hi, Sergeant, what are you doing here? I didn't expect to see you again."

The senior cop had removed his uniform jacket, but even in short sleeves he was wilting beneath the brutal sun. Yet his brown eyes had lost their perpetual sadness and actually twinkled beneath his bushy silver hair.

"Didn't expect to be here again, but we'll be closing up shop in a few hours and then we'll all go home for good."

"No kidding? What will we do without Charlotte's Finest hanging around?" Amanda held out her purse for Jacobs to search.

He ignored the purse, but took the sketchbook from her hands, flipped through the empty pages. "Too bad. I expected to see some interesting drawings, young lady."

"Well, I hope to work on some today." She was so relieved not to be searched that she almost forgot to worry about the police leaving. Their continuing presence had been both a pain and a comfort.

"You're in a good mood today, Sergeant."

"You bet. I have only one month to go now until full retirement and it looks like I'll make it. After this Metrolina gig I'll be riding a desk until I ride off into the sunset."

"Congratulations."

"Thanks, and hey, I almost forgot, I have something for you…" He handed back her sketch pad and dug into his pocket. "This is the new key to your alley door. I already gave copies to the Monroe ladies before they left this morning. I'll give one to Marc Orlando soon as they finish changing the lock on his door, and then I'm outta here."

She absently slid the key into her pocket. "Is Marc here now?" She held her breath. The only reason she'd come today was to see Sara. Sara had spent yesterday helping Marc load his silly bricks, so Amanda assumed she'd help him unload as well.

"Yeah, he's down at the south entrance making a racket. He's the only one in the building, far as I know."

Bummer. Of course, maybe Jacobs simply hadn't noticed Sara? She smiled at the old sergeant and went inside.

"Good luck, ma'am!" he called after her.

"Same to you!" she shouted over her shoulder.

Before ducking into her booth, she peered down the dark hallway and realized how empty the place felt with the other exhibitors gone. The silence was eerie, broken only by the occasional thump of the bricks being offloaded in the distance. Frankly, it gave her the creeps, and she decided on the spot that if Sara wasn't there, she'd go home at once. After all, she could agonize over her drawings while sitting by the lake just as well as she could in a spooky, deserted warehouse.

Once inside the privacy of her own space, she fished the pistol from her undies, stashed it in her purse, and then locked her purse in her desk drawer. Much as she might want to leave early, Amanda knew the cops would definitely search her purse on the way out and she wasn't willing to do the ridiculous bikini stash again. She'd just have to wait until they were gone.

She did a couple of stretches and practiced breathing while she worked up the courage to begin work. Finally, she picked up her sketch pad, deciding it would make her look busy and purposeful, and marched down the silent hallway toward the Orlandos.

The south entrance was propped open, creating a blinding square of white light. The shiny red angles of Marc's F150 pickup truck cut across the square, composing a Cubist painting. His dark head bobbed up and down as he lifted bricks off the tailgate and stacked them on the ground.

Amanda blinked when she stepped out to greet him, and the humidity swamped her. "Hey, Marc, aren't you working too hard? You'll get heat stroke."

He stood upright panting, with sweat streaming down his bare, muscular chest. His face was flushed from exertion and his dark eyes burned.

"What the hell, Amanda?" he barked. "I have a bone to pick with you!"

Before Amanda knew what was happening, he spun around and locked her upper arms in a vise-like grip. The rough texture of his work gloves bit into her skin.

Gasping in surprise, fearing he was about to strike her, Amanda was too scared to protest when he dragged her inside the building. He lifted the tarp to his booth and shoved her beneath it.

"Let go, Marc! What's wrong with you?" She struggled free and shifted behind a table, putting it between them.

He pounded the table with his fist. "I don't know what game you're playing, Amanda, but you better start explaining. Fast."

CHAPTER FORTY-TWO

Sensing violence…

Whatever this was about, she didn't deserve it. She hit the table with her own fist. "What are you talking about, Marc?"

"My sister Sara. What kind of game are you playing with her?"

She was stunned. How much did he know about their relationship, and why was it any of his business?

"Where is Sara? I thought she'd be with you today."

"Sorry to disappoint you, but she's home licking her wounds." He pulled off his gloves, slapped them down on the table, and glared at her.

She glared right back. "What wounds?"

Marc huffed and ran his fingers through his black hair. "You know Sara's been hurt before, and she's not over it yet. What makes you think you can blow into her life and drag her down again?"

Amanda was furious. She was damn sure Sara had said nothing to justify Marc's attitude. "Look, Marc, I don't know what you think you know about Sara and me, but you don't have a clue."

"Why didn't you tell me you were a lesbian?"

"You didn't ask, did you?" This was really too much. Amanda flashed back on the first time she met him. Marc had hit on her, so was he pissed because she'd chosen the wrong twin? She also remembered Lena's implication that Marc's fondness for his sister was somehow incestuous, so maybe he was jealous of Amanda? Neither scenario was pretty.

"Leave her alone, Amanda," he growled.

"Are you threatening me?" she asked, sensing violence.

"Why did you wait so long to tell Detective Molerno how Sara's prints got on the weapon?" He clenched his fists.

"Why did you lie to Molerno about knowing Ben Marsh?" Amanda shot back. "Lena told me you fought with Ben at an office party. You hated him, didn't you?"

Marc gripped the edge of the table and upended it. It almost landed on Amanda's toes. Soda cans, hammer and nails and Marc's gloves toppled to the floor.

Amanda jumped backward in shock, focused on the gloves. Carlson and Maribelle Porter weren't the only ones who could have avoided leaving fingerprints on the tomahawk.

"Jesus, Marc, did you kill him?"

His eyes expanded with an emotion Amanda could not fathom. When he bent down to retrieve the hammer, Carlson Porter strolled into the building, whistling "The Star-Spangled Banner."

He stopped in his tracks. "What's going on in there?" He rolled back the tarp curtain and gaped at them. "Should I call the cops?"

Marc and Amanda froze.

"That won't be necessary," Amanda said at last. "I was just leaving."

She scampered into the hall.

"That young man has a short fuse, miss. You might want to steer clear." Porter's eyes were too large behind his round rimless glasses. His expression was unreadable.

"No problem, I'm fine," she told him.

"Sergeant Jacobs is just outside. I'll fetch him."

Amanda was torn, but she didn't want Porter or Jacobs interfering. At the same time, she was badly shaken, unsure what had just happened between her and Marc.

"Look, here he comes now…" Porter crossed his plump arms over his pigeon chest. Today he wore black shorts, sandals, and a white short sleeved dress shirt buttoned up to his pink chin. Amanda decided he looked more like a penguin than a pigeon.

As Jacobs approached, he was more wilted and less ebullient than he'd been an hour ago, yet his spirits were still high.

"We're all done, folks, so I came to say good-bye." The sergeant peeked into the Orlandos' space, where Marc was still in suspended animation with the hammer in his hand. Seemingly finding nothing out of the ordinary, Jacobs tossed him a key. "All doors are now secure, so my job is done."

As Jacobs walked away, Porter's mouth opened, then closed. Whatever he intended to say, he swallowed. They both watched in silence as the last two police officers climbed into their patrol car and drove off.

"Good riddance to bad rubbish," Marc growled from his compound.

CHAPTER FORTY-THREE

A long way, baby…

Porter shrugged, then waddled into his booth, where he resumed whistling.

Amanda stood perfectly still just inside the shade of the south entrance, her heart pounding so hard she wondered if she should take an aspirin. Rachel had convinced her to carry the pills in her purse to ward off a heart attack, should the need arise. But Amanda was only twenty-eight years old, unlikely to expire from a bum ticker, and besides, her purse was at the far end of the building, locked in her desk.

Get a grip. As she struggled to understand what had just transpired, she saw her sketch pad splayed open on the gravel beside Marc's truck. She must have dropped it there when Marc grabbed her arms.

When she ventured outside and bent to pick it up, the relentless sun beat down on her head and she was suddenly dizzy. Jesus Christ, what was wrong with her? Was she destined to faint and die on the spot?

Disgusted by her infirmities, Amanda moved back into the building, where the temperature still topped ninety degrees.

Yes, she'd had only a few hours' sleep, she'd consumed only toast and black coffee for breakfast. Thanks to her confusing, intense lovemaking with Sara and the finality of her breakup with Rachel, she was running on emotional empty. The violent encounter with Marc didn't help. But mostly she really badly needed to pee.

She glanced wistfully at the public restrooms, now locked since the cops were gone. So her only option was the exhibitors' private bathroom, which she'd avoided ever since the trouble began. To access it, Amanda was forced to pass through the Thigpen booth and endure Porter's glare of disapproval, but having no choice, she did so.

Fumbling with her key ring, including its many new additions, she found the one that worked and locked herself inside with the hook and eye Marc had installed. It seemed like a lifetime ago.

Sinking gratefully onto the toilet seat, she buried her face in her hands and attempted to organize her thoughts, starting with the most troubling: why was Sara "licking her wounds," as Marc had said? Had Amanda hurt or upset her in some way? She'd expected her to be at Metrolina today, if for no other reason than to return Amanda's cell phone. Surely Sara had found it by now, and as everyone knew, no woman could live without her phone.

If, for instance, Amanda had her phone at that very moment, she'd call Sara and ask her what the hell was going on.

She finished her business, yanked the light chain above the sink, and saw her two old friends—the antique posters she'd so admired. She recalled saying to the sassy ladies in the 1940s ads, "We've come a long way, baby." The framed pieces brought a smile, even today.

But as Amanda soaped her hands, she realized something was different about them. Before, the sexy blonde drinking a classic Coke had hung on the left, while the pretty brunette in pink plastic rollers had been on the right. Today they were switched around. She was certain of this because before, the girls had faced one another, now they looked in opposite directions. This was way wrong.

Unable to stop herself from fixing the out of kilter posters, she reached up and removed the blonde from the wall. She glanced at the backing, as any framer would, and noticed the piece had a gold label from a Charlotte art shop which, no doubt, had gone out of business decades ago. She placed it on the floor.

She removed the brunette holding a Sunbeam hair dryer, and again checked the backing. No gold label. Very strange. Instead of the peeling paper and stained cardboard one would expect, Amanda saw that someone had recently stapled a sheet of modern printing paper to the backside of the frame. Also, she could feel the outline of something inserted beneath the paper.

What on earth? Before she could control them, her fingernails gently lifted one end of each staple and swiveled it outward, so that the sides and lower edge of the paper could be lifted intact. Knowing full well she was committing a trespass, she carefully slid her fingers up and removed the object tucked within.

It was one of those frosted protector sheets. On one side Amanda found a plain leaf of acid-free paper; on the other, hinged to the paper in all its faded glory, was the Lincoln-Davis letter!

She covered her mouth and choked back her cry of surprise, then sank back down on the toilet seat. Her hands were shaking so badly she almost dropped the precious document.

Dear God in heaven!

Arguably, one of the owners was whistling right outside the door. But to put a fine point on it, it had been Michael Thigpen who bought the insurance for the letter. She could run to Marc with her discovery but the idea made her sick to her stomach. Only the police were trustworthy, but they had abandoned the search and left the building, exactly what the thief had been waiting for.

Her brain short-circuiting, incapable of rational thought, she slid the treasure deep between the pages of her sketch pad. With trembling fingers, she bent the staples back against the sheet of backing paper so that at a glance nothing appeared amiss, and then she hung the posters back on the wall as she had found them.

Buying time, she flushed the toilet again, and with all the poise she could muster, picked up her pad and calmly exited the bathroom. Naturally Carlson Porter was still there, sitting at his desk, watching the bathroom door with a snarly look on his face. His head followed her as she passed, so Amanda smiled and waggled her fingers to reassure him. Reassure him of what? That her long delay in the bathroom was just a woman thing?

Determined to keep from running, Amanda moved north up the hall, honing in on her own booth.

CHAPTER FORTY-FOUR

Marc's game...

Halfway up the hall, Amanda stopped to think. If she retrieved her purse, ran to Moby, and drove the hell away as she was planning to do, when she turned it over to the cops, she'd need to do some mighty fast talking to convince them she hadn't stolen it in the first place, then gotten cold feet.

After all, the obscenely high value of the letter gave everyone a motive. It had been Amanda's utility door left open and she'd certainly had opportunity. Her prints were all over the poster frames and, with a little digging, the police would find out she'd once been a custom framer, making the hiding place a natural choice for her.

She clutched the sketch pad tight to her chest and began to hyperventilate. She had witnessed the fight between Sara and Ben, and if Marc, in all his fury, chose to share what he knew about her intimate relationship with Sara, God forbid, the cops might even like her for the murder.

Feeling faint again, Amanda knew she dare not leave the premises with the letter, and she knew she needed help. She must call Detective Molerno immediately. The only public phone she knew about, the one Ben had supposedly used to call a cab that fateful night, was in the parking lot south of the building. To get there quickly, she had to pass by Porter and Marc again.

So be it. Amanda turned and retraced her steps. Each footfall sounded like a thunderclap in the dark deserted space, and the voyage was never-ending. Praying to sneak out unnoticed, she crept toward the square of bright light, the planes of the red truck glinting in the sun, and offered up thanks when she saw Porter was not in his booth.

She was almost clear when a large dark silhouette burst into the light. Marc had emerged from behind his F150, a brick in each hand. Although she couldn't see his face, his posture projected pure menace.

"Where do you think you're going, Amanda?"

His tone, though outwardly calm, implied a threat.

She tried to push past him. "I need to use a phone."

But he blocked her. "I bet you do. You left your cell at Sara's the other night. In fact, she gave it to me so I could return it."

"You have my phone? So why the hell didn't you give it to me?"

"I never got a chance. You were too busy accusing me of murder."

It was a standoff. Amanda figured she had two choices: try to squeeze past him and risk getting crowned by a brick, or play Marc's game—whatever that was.

"So, you want to give me my phone now?" She decided the game was a better choice.

He considered his options, then finally put both bricks down on the ground. "Sure, why not. It's in my toolbox. Let's go get it."

Suddenly he again grasped her arm with one enormous gloved hand, then propelled her around the corner and into his booth. She tripped over a stack of bricks just inside the dark space, dropped her sketch pad on his floor, and quickly panicked. Fortunately the pad did not open to the stolen letter, so she offered up another prayer of thanks.

"Take it easy, I won't bite." Marc handed her the pad and helped her up. "C'mon, my toolbox is back in my studio."

She desperately did not want to follow him into the workspace but had no choice. As he herded her forward she saw the shiny new key in his pass-through door. When they entered, she smelled the clay, the oil, the dust. All her senses were hyper-aware as he guided her toward his workbench.

She managed to slip around the bench, putting it between them as Marc removed his gloves and opened his steel box.

"I know it's in here somewhere..." He lifted out screwdrivers, pliers and a razor-sharp chisel.

Amanda didn't like the way he grasped the chisel in his right hand.

"You hurt my feelings, Amanda. Women have called me ugly names before, but no one's ever called me a killer."

She especially didn't like the manic glitter in his black eyes. "I'm sorry, I didn't mean it."

"Yes, you did."

As Marc moved around the table, inching toward her, she started scoping out an escape route, wondering if she could run to her own studio door without tripping over the many impediments looming in her path.

She wished Marc had turned on the lights, wished she had a lit welding torch in her hands, but mostly wished someone would come to her rescue.

"Please leave me alone, Marc!" Her plea was a pathetic little peep in the emptiness.

At the same time, she saw movement behind Marc's head as someone new slipped into the room. Amanda couldn't identify the person in the shadows, but she was grateful for the intervention.

"Help!" she shouted. This time her voice projected loud and clear.

CHAPTER FORTY-FIVE

Lifeblood…

Marc spun around and lifted his weapon just as the newcomer rushed forward. In that instant Amanda saw it was only Carlson Porter, but she'd take any help in this crisis. She also saw Porter was wearing his silly white gloves and waving something back and forth in a bizarre sweeping motion. Too late, she realized it was a sword.

"Put that down before you hurt yourself, asshole!" Marc shouted as he lunged at the little man, but Porter kept coming.

Before she could process what was happening, Porter raised the sword and came down hard, just missing Marc's head, but burying the blade in his shoulder.

Marc screamed in pain, dropped the chisel, and fell to his knees just as Porter moved in for a fatal second blow.

"Stop!" Amanda couldn't believe this was happening. She picked up the open toolbox and hurled it at Porter.

It hit him on the right arm, deflecting the sword from Marc but enraging Porter, who charged toward Amanda.

"Run, Amanda, the man's crazy!" Marc stuck out one leg, tripping Porter, who fell into a pile of rough cedar boards and dropped the sword.

As Porter flailed on the lumber, Amanda found the chisel, her heart knocking wildly inside her chest cavity. While her feet told her to run, what was left of her mind knew that Porter would kill Marc unless she stopped him.

Sure enough, Porter located a hammer on the floor and staggered off the pile toward Marc, who was bleeding profusely and still pleading with Amanda to run. Unable to prevent it, she watched in horror as Porter lifted the hammer in a vicious arc and brought it down on Marc's forehead.

Marc groaned once, wilted backward, then moved no more.

Amanda's scream raised the birds in the rafters. They took frenzied flight, beating their wings against the girders in a desperate bid to escape.

Amanda, frozen in terror, knew exactly how they felt. Lifting one hand in a gesture of peace, she held the sketch pad aloft in the other.

"I have what you want, Mr. Porter…" His eyes bugged and followed her every move as she slid the pad onto the workbench. "Take it, please, and let me call an ambulance!"

He nodded and smiled, but his expression conveyed only menace. Suddenly, Amanda knew he would kill her too. He couldn't afford to leave a witness alive. Instead he'd concoct some insane story blaming Marc and her for their mutual deaths and the previous crimes. Judging by his luck so far, he'd get away with it.

"I'm begging you," she whimpered. "Let me go, and I won't tell anyone!"

Even to Amanda's ears, her groveling sounded preposterous and disgusting. By his maniacal laugh, Porter agreed. When he threw the hammer at her, she lifted her hands in defense, but the tool hit her hard on the collarbone, leaving a bloody stain on her blouse. It was Marc's blood, blood of Sara's twin brother.

Beyond the shriek of pain that radiated through her upper body, Amanda felt a jolt of pure fury as Porter rushed her. Falling to her knees, she waited until Porter was upon her, then thrust the chisel as hard as she could into his upper thigh. The blade held there for a second, then clattered to the floor.

Porter squealed like a stuck pig and fumbled at the wound with his pudgy hands. Amanda hoped she had not hit his femoral artery; she didn't want to kill anybody. But she sure as hell wanted to slow him down, and took the opportunity to run for her life.

If she could only make it to her door and find the right key, she could get into her booth and lock the monster out. Arms outstretched, she groped through the gloom, putting distance between them as the tenor of Porter's squealing shifted to an angry bellow. She was okay until she tripped over Jenny's potter's wheel and hit concrete.

She heard the middle finger of her left hand break, but compared to the queasy agony in her collarbone, the sudden flash of pain was a blinding insult. Fueled by a surge of adrenaline unlike anything she'd ever experienced, Amanda dug into her pocket and found her keychain.

Speeding across the floor on all fours, she hallucinated that she was a dog, limping on its left front paw. She was nonetheless able to get up on her hind legs and twist the correct key in the lock, and the door swung inward.

She was the prey, and her hunter was moving slow. That was good. But suddenly there was an explosion, and the wooden molding of the doorframe shattered one foot from her face, sending a barrage of splinters into her cheek, narrowly missing her eye.

Armed hunter, not so good. As another bullet hit the opened door, Amanda dove forward in sheer panic. Holding her wounded left hand folded across her body like a broken wing, she rolled into her fall.

As she snaked across the floor toward her desk, she heard Porter closing in. He too was hampered by dark obstacles, and she heard him trip. He cursed at the top of his lungs and let a third bullet fly. That one hit harmlessly somewhere out in the studio.

Sweet Jesus, help me!

She twice inserted wrong keys into her desk drawer, then giggled hysterically when the next one—third time's the charm—actually worked. She dragged out her purse, found her Raven pistol, and quickly pushed off the safety.

Hoping Porter had only three bullets left, Amanda still freaked when she saw him framed in her doorway. She rolled across the floor and took shelter behind her *Wing Chair*. The fourth bullet ricocheted off a chrome bumper.

She took careful aim, but choked. She had never shot at a live target, let alone another human being. As she hesitated, she saw a burst of light as the fifth bullet took flight and lodged somewhere between her ribs.

Stunned by pain and disbelief, Amanda's vision blurred as she sank to the floor. She saw him thrash at his trigger, his gun's wheel turning to no effect at all. Either he had a six-shooter that hadn't been fully loaded, or it was a five-shooter.

Even as her lifeblood drained away, Amanda held her breath and aimed, pretending he was a paper target, and when he moved, she fired again and again.

After that, there was only black.

CHAPTER FORTY-SIX

Uncharted waters...

The underwater world left her helpless as a fetus in the uterus, so she floated through the murky liquid tethered to the umbilical cords feeding her saline, nutrients and antibiotics. Unaware of the passage of time punctuated only by sharp sensations of pain, by human voices slow and garbled as an old-fashioned 45RPM record played at 33RPM, she swam through the uncharted waters oblivious to anything but the effort to breathe and the rhythm of her heart.

Occasionally she recognized an image, a sound, or a thought from her former life. But these soon faded. Gradually the tangibles came more frequently and lingered longer until she woke up and gazed into the same face she saw when she left the womb.

"Am I dead?" she asked her mama through parched lips.

"No, honey, you are very much alive!"

Then she knew she was Amanda, and the woman holding her right hand was her mother. She didn't understand why there were tears in her mother's eyes, or why her left hand was in a splint, or why her upper body and ribs were bound up in bandages.

"You're alive, and you're a hero!" said the tall man standing behind her mother. He was smiling, his aura was gentle, and after several heartbeats, she remembered he was Trout.

As she shifted her gaze back and forth between them, the nightmare images flooded back. She saw blood pouring from a sword wound and a hammer crushing the young man's head.

"Is Marc dead?" The name came unbidden.

"He's doing okay," her mother said. "In fact, he's here in this hospital, one floor down. I understand his shoulder is healing but the concussion was the main concern. They say he's talking now, and making sense."

Amanda was deeply relieved. Although she couldn't remember details, she now knew Marc was not her enemy. She saw a dark warehouse filled with hurtful obstacles and sharp weapons. She recalled falling and stabbing the monster with a chisel. But when she recalled the bullets and finding her gun, she felt the recoil in her hand and saw the man fall.

"I killed him, didn't I?" Suddenly she was sobbing. She sensed her mother and Trout looking at one another, trying to decide how much to divulge.

"Mr. Porter's in this hospital too," Diana said softly. "He's under heavy guard in the psych ward surgery. He lost a lot of blood, and for a while it was touch and go. If you had hit his femoral artery he'd be dead, and I know you didn't want that, honey."

"You nailed him in both shoulders, Mandy Bear," Trout added. "You're a darn good shot, but neither hit was fatal."

Thank God! Amanda closed both eyes and felt warm tears leaking from their corners. She was exhausted, hardly able to form words or stay awake.

Her mother touched her arm. "Before you drift off, honey, we have some good news. We got a call from that nice man at Wells Fargo. He said take all the time you need to complete the drawings and the commission. They think you're awesome, and they'll wait as long as it takes."

"And the Lease Office from Metrolina sent a letter refunding all your rent, inviting you to stay for free," Trout added. "You know I want you to work up in my garage instead, but that's up to you. You're a celebrity, girl, and everyone wants a little piece of you."

It all sounded good, but Amanda would have to think about it later. "How's the family?" she managed drowsily.

"Right now Matthew and I are the only ones allowed to see you. But the police have been roaming the hallways, hoping to speak with you as soon as you woke up. Is that okay?"

It hurt to nod.

Trout's deep voice was the last thing she heard. "Take all the time you need, darlin', those vultures can wait."

CHAPTER FORTY-SEVEN

Molerno…

She knew it was late afternoon by the way the sun slanted through the venetian blinds and hit her in the eyes. She pushed the call button, and a nurse appeared almost immediately.

"Look who's awake! Lord, child, you've been dead to the world since yesterday morning."

The middle-aged woman with chocolate hands was usually her night nurse. Amanda liked her, the way she anticipated her needs. Like now, as she twisted the blinds closed.

"What day is it?"

The nurse pointed at a big white board on the wall with the date and the name of her shift nurses written in erasable black magic marker. Amanda squinted, but her vision was still blurry and she couldn't make it out.

"It's Thursday, June 25th, in the year 2015. And you've been here six long days, young lady. My name's Rhonda, case you forgot."

"Thanks, Rhonda."

"You feel like a little soup? The only food you been eating lately comes through them tubes, so I know you must be hungry."

The idea made Amanda nauseated—mostly. "Do you have a cherry Popsicle?"

Rhonda laughed. "I think we could find one of those." She pointed to the colorful vases of flowers placed around the room. "You've got lots of friends. These flowers have been coming in all week. And you've got a big fan club here. The staff's been saving all the newspaper clippings in a scrapbook for you."

Amanda didn't know what to say. None of it quite made sense, but she smiled.

"And I hate to say it, but that detective's pacing the hall outside. You up to seeing him yet?"

She wasn't sure, but didn't know how to say no.

"How do I look?"

Rhonda cocked her head. "Not too bad, considering. I'll fetch a mirror."

Amanda saw angry red marks on her left cheek, like she'd been scratched by a cat. "What's this?" She touched them with her good hand.

"They dug some splinters out, but you won't have a scar. Here, let me brush your hair…"

She submitted to Rhonda's gentle touch, and since there wasn't much hair to deal with, decided she didn't look too bad after all—like a duckling after a fight with a turtle.

"Okay, I guess I'll see the detective."

Rhonda left, and when she returned she had an unwrapped cherry Popsicle sitting in a white Styrofoam cup. She also had Molerno in tow. His suit was rumpled, his cheap tie tugged loose from around his muscular neck. Italian street fighter.

"Molerno!" The name came with a bitter taste in her mouth as all the bad memories crowded back.

He pulled up a chair and took possession of the Popsicle cup. "You look awful, Rittenhouse." He grinned, found the remote control, and raised the head of her bed.

"Eat first, talk later." He yanked a length of paper towel from the roll on her table, tucked a bib into her gown, and began feeding her.

Normally she would have resisted and resented, but the icy flavor was so damn good, she gave up and enjoyed. Molerno's bedside manner wasn't half bad. She wondered if he had little kids at home.

"That freak Porter's been shooting his mouth off. He told us you stole the letter, hid it behind the poster frame, and then tried to sneak it out in a sketchbook."

Her mouth was stuffed, so she couldn't respond.

"He explained how you tried to butcher Marc Orlando with a sword, then conked him with a hammer."

Molerno inserted another icy chunk. She'd gag if she tried to speak.

"This last bit should put you behind bars for a hundred years," Molerno continued gleefully. "Porter described how you tried to kill him—first with the bloody chisel, and then you shot him twice. Good thing he was armed with his rusty old Colt .45, or he'd be a dead man today."

He paused while she desperately swallowed. As soon as her brain freeze subsided, Amanda choked out the words:

"He's lying!"

"Really?" Molerno roughly wiped her lips with another scrap of paper towel. "Marc Orlando says he's lying too. Soon as he was able to talk, Orlando said Porter was a fucking piece of dog shit who wouldn't know the truth from the hole in his ass—or words to that effect."

Amanda laughed, but the sound came out more like a cough. "What do *you* think, Detective?"

He rubbed the afternoon shadow on his jaw. "The shrinks have a word for what ails Mr. Porter. They call it *projection*. They figure he's conjured up every piece of criminal crap he's done, then blamed it on you. Do you agree with the shrinks, Rittenhouse?"

CHAPTER FORTY-EIGHT

To finally have answers…

Of course Amanda agreed with the shrinks and decided the question didn't even merit an answer.

"It seems clear Mr. Porter stole the letter," she said. "But how did Ben Marsh die?"

Molerno threw the Styrofoam cup in the trash. "The murder is the only thing Porter did not blame on you. But his wife Maribelle lost no time pointing her finger in your direction."

"Maribelle? I don't understand! Both Porters were there that night and as far as I know, they were still there when I left. Why would Maribelle implicate me?"

"I don't think she dislikes you any more or less than she dislikes the whole of humanity, but after the shootout, you were a convenient scapegoat. Point is, Maribelle's accusation perfectly fit my working theory, so I arrested her for murder."

Amanda couldn't believe her ears.

"I believed all along that Ben's death was an unintended consequence of the theft," Molerno continued. "I think he might have left the premises in a cab that night, but he then doubled back and sneaked into Building 16 to confront Sara Orlando.

"We may never know how he got in undetected—could have been through your alley door, could have blended in with the late customers and hid—but he was in the Orlando booth when the Porters took the letter from the frame."

"How can you possibly know all that?"

"I know because Carlson Porter turned on his wife, or more accurately, he offered information when he should have kept his big mouth shut. As soon as we arrested Maribelle, with very little cause the man imploded and told us his wife never meant to hurt Ben. He said the whole thing was an accident."

"Maribelle killed him? I don't believe it!"

"Ben Marsh was drunk and primed for a fight. When he saw the pair lifting the letter, he confronted them rather violently, and Maribelle bashed him with the tomahawk. It took both husband and wife to haul him into that window seat."

"But why would they leave the thing buried in his chest?"

Molerno shrugged. He walked to the window and looked out at the Charlotte skyline. "Who knows? Maybe they were too squeamish to pull it out. Or since they were both wearing gloves, they figured they'd never be tied to the weapon. Or maybe they were stupid…"

"Or maybe they remembered the incident when Sara handled the tomahawk just hours before and decided to frame her for the murder," Amanda finished bitterly.

The speculation brought on a massive headache. She was overdue for her next morphine fix, but above all, she was mightily relieved to finally have answers.

"What will happen to them?"

Molerno walked back and sat on the edge of her bed. "That will be up to the judge and jury but I guarantee they won't see the light of day for a very long time. If they weren't such nasty people, it would be kind of sad. Obviously they were tired of being under Michael Thigpen's heavy thumb and you can't blame them."

"I can," Amanda commented angrily. "And by the way, how come we all made it to the hospital in time? Why didn't we die?"

He barked out a laugh. "Believe it or not, the three of you made a lot of noise. I'm thinking it was a cross between the shoot-out at the O.K. Corral and the assault on Ramadi. Anyway, you rousted Jack and June Harris from their mobile home and they came to the rescue. June administered first aid, Jack called for the troops. Long story short, those two sorry shits saved your lives."

Amanda had to think about that. It seemed she'd have to revise her opinion about the Harrises. In spite of the dead dove, they would never again be "sorry shits" in her estimation.

But as the enormity, the horror of the brush with death took hold of her mind, she longed to sink back into oblivion. She closed her eyes.

"Hey, don't check out on me just yet." Molerno tapped her sore collarbone. "You're not out of the woods yet, Rittenhouse."

She opened one eye.

"Far as I can tell, you aren't licensed to carry a concealed weapon in North Carolina. That's a misdemeanor, you know."

She knew, and she didn't care, and by the chuckle in his voice, neither did Molerno. She closed her one eye and let go.

CHAPTER FORTY-NINE

Obergefell v. Hodges...

The next morning Rhonda was on duty again. After supervising Amanda's eating of oatmeal, juice and toast, she unhooked her patient from the various clear plastic bottles hung on the aluminum Christmas tree. Amanda was deemed ready to use the bathroom and shower, and she was also relieved of her hated Foley catheter.

"Are you sure I'm ready?" Still hurting, Amanda couldn't quite believe her good fortune.

"Oh, I'm real sure. Doc says you're cleared to see your friends, not just family. Now family's gonna understand you looking raggedy, but friends are more picky. We gotta clean you up, girl."

"What friends?" According to her mother, Ginny, Trev and Lissa, also Liz and Danny had been pushing to visit her, but they were more like family.

"Well, for starters, there's that girl who's been hanging outside your door ever since you got here."

"What girl?" Amanda held her breath.

"Don't rightly know her name, but her brother came to the hospital same time you did." Rhonda licked her lips. "And her brother's a handsome dude. All the nurses fight to give him his sponge bath."

Sara! During the long days of semiconsciousness, she'd felt Sara's presence hovering just beyond reach and longed to bring her into clear focus. She'd sensed Sara's image at the end of the tunnel would speed her healing, but she didn't know where she stood with her.

"Have you seen the girl in the hallway today?"

"Sure enough, she was there when I came in. I told her you might be seeing her soon."

Amanda's heart jumped into her throat and fluttered like a captive bird. "So how soon can I take that shower?"

She was ready by lunchtime—clean, shampooed, and dressed in the freshly laundered shorts and large blouse her mother had brought for her. It took some fancy maneuvering to ease her splinted hand and bandaged torso into the blouse, but Rhonda managed to get her decently buttoned.

Rhonda admired her handiwork. "Now don't you look fine."

"Do I have to meet Sara in this room? Isn't there someplace else, outside maybe?"

Her nurse frowned. "Well, it's a beautiful day, and I reckon you won't catch a chill if I wheel you out to the roof garden."

"I can walk under my own steam."

"No, ma'am, I don't think so." She gathered up and lowered Amanda into a wheelchair. "Besides, it's against regulations."

Before Amanda could arrange her emotions, she was rolled out of her room, down a busy hallway and past a nurses' station, then out through an automatic door leading to the roof. She was bombarded with stimuli she had not experienced in what seemed like years: hot sun on her head, wind on her face, the faint odor of tar coming off the asphalt.

"I'll go find that girl and bring her here. Then I'll leave you two alone."

Amanda wasn't ready, didn't know how to act or what to say. But before she could worry too long, Sara was there—

standing right in front of her. She wore the same emerald-green blouse she'd worn the night they made love. She stood in partial shadow, with one shard of light cascading like water down the gentle curves of her breasts and hips as she moved in close.

"My sweet Amanda. I am so sorry this happened to you." The cameo of her beautiful face was creased in worry, but her full red lips parted in a smile just before she kissed her.

It took Amanda's breath away. "What are you doing?" she gasped when the kiss ended. "Someone will see us!"

"So what if they do? We're all the rage."

Amanda had no idea what she was talking about, but the amazing kiss was quite an ice-breaker.

"Please, Sara, I need to ask you something. The day Marc and I got hurt, the day he came alone to Metrolina, he said you were home 'licking your wounds.' What did he mean? Had I done something to hurt you?"

She thought about it. "I don't know. Marc can be a jerk sometimes. But since he's been in the hospital he's told me a hundred times how sorry he is about the way he treated you that day. He thinks I'll break to pieces like a little china doll if someone rejects me. Marc needs to get a life."

In her wildest dreams, Amanda could not imagine anyone rejecting Sara, but perhaps that was a different story, one Sara would share in time. "But why were you 'licking your wounds'?"

Sara thought some more, and then she broke out laughing, sending the sound of the Liberty Bell echoing across the roof of the Carolina's Medical Center. "Yes, as a matter of fact, I was licking my wounds, but not in the way Marc led you to believe. Thing is, I'm a klutz, Amanda. That day I helped my brother, I dropped a load of antique bricks on my foot and broke two toes. I've been limping around ever since."

Amanda hadn't noticed, but when Sara held up her left foot it had a splint on it very much like the one on Amanda's left hand.

"We're a sorry pair," Amanda observed.

"Maybe so, but we've got a lot to celebrate."

"What are you talking about?"

Sara gave her a strange look. "Haven't you been watching TV?"

"We don't get TV in Critical Care."

"Oh, sorry, I guess not." Sara giggled. "Then maybe I better fill you in…" She located a white plastic lawn chair, dragged it so close their knees touched.

As the sun climbed directly overhead, Sara explained, "This morning the Supreme Court announced a decision. The case was *Obergefell v. Hodges*. Five to four, the justices affirmed that same-sex couples are entitled to marry nationwide. Can you believe it, Amanda?" Sara shouted. "Marriage equality is now the law of the land!"

"Oh my God!" In spite of the punishing heat, a chill passed through Amanda's body and she was numb with joy. "I thought they wouldn't decide that case until the fall." And she'd honestly never dared hope the verdict would be favorable.

"I know, it's awesome! I never thought this could happen in our lifetime."

"Neither did I." Amanda remained numb as Sara took her one good hand into both of hers. "What will happen, do you think?"

Sara was jubilant. "What do you think? Couples all over the nation will be getting licenses and tying the knot by the end of the day."

"Folks who are into relationships and commitment, you mean."

"Sure, those crazy folks." Sara tossed her hair. "To each his own, but at least we now have the option."

"Yes, we have the option." Amanda didn't know where to go with any of this. She certainly wasn't ready for wedding bells, but now the future seemed limitless.

A faraway look entered Sara's green eyes as she peered out over the edge, into the blue sky above the Charlotte skyline. "What about you, Mandy, would you ever get married?"

Amanda gazed at her, smiling. "I don't know. I guess we'll have to wait and see."

Other Books by Kate Merrill

Romance
Northern Lights (as Christie Cole)
Flames of Summer

Diana Rittenhouse Mystery Series
A Lethal Listing
Blood Brothers
Crimes of Commission
Dooley Is Dead
Buyer Beware

Amanda Rittenhouse Mystery Series
Murder at Metrolina
Homicide in Hatteras (coming soon)

Bella Books, Inc.

Women. Books. Even Better Together.

P.O. Box 10543
Tallahassee, FL 32302

Phone: 800-729-4992
www.bellabooks.com